D0330684

the
children
and the
wolves

the
children
and the
wolves

adam rapp

CANDLEWICK PRESS

Copyright © 2012 by Adam Rapp

The author gratefully acknowledges permission to reprint the poem *Falling Life* by Zachary Schomburg from *Scary, No Scary* (Black Ocean, 2009).

First edition 2012

Library of Congress Cataloging-in-Publication Data

Rapp, Adam.
The children and the wolves / Adam Rapp. — 1st ed.
p. cm.
Summary: Abducted by teen genius Bounce and her drifter friends Wiggins and Orange, three-year-old Frog seems content to eat cereal and play a video game about wolves all day — a game that parallels the reality around her — until Wiggins is overcome by guilt and tension and takes action.
ISBN 978-0-7636-5337-8
[1. Kidnapping — Fiction. 2. Conduct of life — Fiction.
3. Emotional problems — Fiction. 4. Single-parent families — Fiction.
5. Drug abuse — Fiction. 6. Illinois — Fiction.] I. Title.
PZ7.R18133Chi   2011
[Fic] — dc23   2011013676

11 12 13 14 15 16 BVG 10 9 8 7 6 5 4 3 2 1

Printed in Berryville, VA, U.S.A.

This book was typeset in Photina.

Candlewick Press
99 Dover Street
Somerville, Massachusetts 02144

visit us at www.candlewick.com

You are in a very high tree.

If you jump
you will live a full life
while falling.

You will get married
to a hummingbird

and raise beautiful part–
hummingbirds.

You will die of cancer
in mid–air.

I will not lie.
It will be painful.

You are a brave little boy
or girl.

—Zachary Schomburg

Wiggins

Dirty Diana soaks her feet in bleach. She puts Clorox in a bucket of hot water and soaks them during Craig Ferguson.

They itch, she says. The fuckers itch.

She's a pediatrician nurse and she says it's okay. Nurses know science and medicine and how to kill a fungus. I never get funguses so I don't got no worries about that. Once I got a cold but it went away cause I drank a thing of Tabasco sauce.

Dirty Diana's one hand always twitches after she puts her feet in the water. I couldn't tell you what her other hand is doing. It's like that hand is always hiding something.

About the bleach she says, It's cheaper than the sprays. The sprays and those phony powders.

She says it's okay that there was a dead bird in the kitchen too. It was black and it had a eye like a ninja. This was like a year ago. It just appeared next to the stove like the kitchen imagined it. Sometimes the refrigerator hums like it's thinking. I have a feeling that it dreams. If it has a nightmare it could poison all your food.

Sometimes I worry that the refrigerator will start talking to me when no one's around. Wiggins, it'll say. I know what you're up to, you bad little boy. You fucking gangbanging thug.

I'm not no gangbanger but the refrigerator prolly thinks I am.

Dirty Diana's my mom and we got the same weird eyes.

She'll say, They gave us hazel eyes and little pygmy bladders, Wiggins.

She's short but she ain't no pygmy. Pygmies are nigger midgets and we ain't no niggers, we're white as paper.

And about Dirty Diana's bladder:

Sometimes I can hear her on the toilet. She don't go for a long time and sometimes she cries and turns on the shower to hide the emotions of it, but I don't have those problems. Once I pissed longer than a TV commercial. It was a advertisement about Ford Truck Toughness and I outpissed it. Sometimes I piss the bed, specially when I'm rolling. Oxycotton can make you lazy, I'll admit it. I've pissed the bed and slept in it like a derelict. When you're rolling you'll let yourself get away with just about anything.

Dirty Diana's eyes are smaller than mine cause she don't hardly sleep. Most of the time it's like she can barely keep them open. Sometimes she'll close them when she's sitting at the kitchen table and they'll start swimming around all weird under her eyelids.

I notice eyes a lot. Like the lady who drove my school bus, Ms. Herbert. Her eyes are scrunched and blue. Or the man down the hall with his little dog that looks like a rat with upside-down teeth. The man's name is Prisby Pound and his eyes are green and they look like someone pushed them too far into his head with their thumbs. His TV's always on the Home Shopping channel. When he turns it off it's like he's dead. Or like you'd open his door and there would just be black space with maybe a huge floating rock. No floors or walls or nothing.

I like drawing eyes and I like studying one and then the other one. Most people got a good and a bad eye. Or a big eye and a small eye. Or a mean eye and a nice eye.

Animals too.

About that bird in my kitchen:

It looked like someone busted it open and flinged it at the stove. You could see its heart and stomach meats. It was next to the

3

stove for a few days and the bugs were all over it. It was scientific to watch. Flies and ants and a little white worm wiggling into its heart. Eventually Dirty Diana picked it up with salad tongs and dropped it in the trash. Then I took the trash down and put it in the dumpster.

You're a good man, Wiggins, she said when I came back.

She was smoking and eating a purple popsicle.

My little garbage man, she said.

But Dirty Diana don't know that before I put the bird in the dumpster I pulled its head off. It was easier than I thought, but I'm strong for my skinniness.

When I got back to the apartment I plopped the birdhead in the toilet and watched it float for a while. I kept waiting for that ninja eye to tell me something.

What? I said to it. What?

But it didn't say shit so I flushed it.

My hands smelled like deadness and I kept smelling them for the rest of the night.

Dirty Diana cleaned the bird smears with the same bleach she uses to soak her feet.

4

Fucking crow in my kitchen, she said, down on her hands and knees, scrubbing.

How poetic, she said.

I'm pretty sure it flew in through her bedroom window cause she always forgets to close it and it don't got no screen. We've been infested with mosquitoes all summer. She says that that's why she sleeps on the couch now There's a shape in it like her body.

Fucking mosquitoes divebombing in my ears, she'll say. After two shifts of whining kids that's the last thing I need.

Her room looks like it got scrambled by thieves. It smells like cigarettes and her armpits. She used to read romance novels and they're scattered on the floor. She don't read no more, though. She mostly watches Craig Ferguson and smokes weed and claws at her hairy little troll feet.

The only thing she keeps on a hanger is her white nurse's uniform. She's got two of them. She washes them in the sink and hangs them on a hook on the other side of the bathroom door. You can hear them dripping on the floor all night. I imagine a animal bleeding and a puddle of blood. The floor's always soaked in the morning.

When she wakes up, her face looks like it got punched.

Sometimes I'll watch her sleep.

Diana, I'll whisper. Hey, Diana.

I try and imagine being pulled out of her at the hospital. Did she reach between her legs and yank me out with her own hands or did they have to use those huge hospital tools you hear about? Like a hook or a shovel?

Sometimes I imagine myself in a pickle jar, floating in science juice. Barely alive with see-through skin. My heart like a little white raisin.

I think something happened to me when I was born. Like maybe I got bit by a spider or I slept too close to the microwave.

From my room I can hear Dirty Diana scratching her troll feet to Craig Ferguson. She's in love with him.

His accent, she says. I just love his accent.

I think the bleach only makes the itching worse but she's the nurse and she knows about sanitation. Once she made me wash my hair with this brown stuff.

It's for lice, she said. Boys get lice and you're a boy.

It smelled like go-cart fuel and burnt behind my ears.

When the scratching stops I know she's asleep and that's when I sneak out to feed the Frog.

Hold it, she told her. If you drop it you'll be sorry.

That was back in May and it's July now. It's been over a hundred degrees lately. You don't never stop sweating. Sometimes I go chill over at the bowling alley with Orange just to be in the air conditioning. He's got a private business arrangement with the guy who sprays the shoes down. Sometimes the manager comes out and tells us to fuck off. His name is Glen and he's got so many acne scars it looks like his face got mangled.

He'll be like, You're not gonna bowl then beat it.
We're gonna bowl, Orange'll say.
Glen'll be like, Then pay for a frigging lane and bowl. Mercury Lanes ain't a cantina, it's a bowling alley.

At night it gets so hot you can smell the fish rotting in the river.

Smells like prostitution, Mr. Merlo says, opening the patio doors. Prostitution and dead puppies.

I think the heat is keeping me from becoming a man. Like it's killing my hormone makers. But I'm not waiting around. I do mannish things anyway. And the thing is that I ain't afraid of nothing. I'd cut myself with my knife just as soon as I'd cut someone else. My knife is deadly sharp and good for stabbing. Bounce gave it to me for my thirteenth birthday. My birthday is April 8th and I'm a Aries, which means I'm a battering ram. I ain't never stabbed nobody, but I've dreamt about it. Like Mexican gangbangers chasing me in the mall.

Good night, Mom, I whisper. Time to feed the Frog.

We keep the Frog in Orange's basement. Orange lives in the yellow condos, on the other side of Piano Road. He's got a upstairs and a basement, but it's only him and his dad living there now. His mom disappeared six months ago. Nobody knows where she is. She worked at the library and had to have one of her breasts removed and lost all her hair and had to wear a cancer wig.

Once I asked Orange where he thought she was.

Who cares, he said. Fucking one-titted freak.

There are stacks of newspapers all over their house. Newspapers and TV Guides and books about alien abduction. Orange's dad was a mailman but something happened to his nervous system and now he's in a wheelchair and can't go up or down stairs, which is cool cause he'll never find the Frog.

Hey, Mr. Merlo, I'll say.

He'll say hey back but he's not all there. He's obese and he's usually rolling. He mostly watches NASCAR and that reality show with Flava Flav and all his ghetto bitches. I like that one, he'll say. The one with the big butt and the teeth.

There's some woods behind the yellow condos and these men live in them and light bomb fires. At night you can see the trees glowing. Orange says the men are part monster.

Get the gringo! they scream.

Get that nasty white bitch!

But then I whirl on them and go at their necks.

Sometimes I'll stab the couch and work it around. The couch or the side of my mattress.

We don't wait for the world, Bounce says. The world has to catch up to us.

The Frog sleeps on the cement floor cause it's cooler than the couch. Even though she's little she sweats like a man. Sometimes when I come down to the basement she's sleeping on the floor like that. Like she fell a hundred feet and got stuck that way.

When I lock the bike chain on her leg she makes a clicking sound with her mouth. It's gotten so I can't tell if it's the lock or her mouth making the sound. She can only move about two feet in any direction, just far enough to reach the couch. The bike chain is connected to a hot-water pipe, so she leans up against it a lot.

I keep the key to the bike chain on a shoelace I wear around my neck.

What's that for? Dirty Diana asked the other night.

Her and her girl Miggy was smoking weed and watching Skinemax. Miggy works at the hospital with her. I was doing push-ups with my shirt off. I can do thirty-five without stopping. My goal is to do a thousand and have huge purple veins.

About the key I was like, It's just a key I found. It's for good luck. Dirty Diana said, You're gonna need plenty of that, crumbum.

At night I take the shoelace from around my neck and sleep with the key in my fist.

Orange

I got the copy machine from Lyde. He gave it to me cause I let him do me.

I'm going to do you proper, he said.

Then he started panting like a dog. His breath smelled like Taco Bell and his lips were quivery. He uses wave activator and it makes his head stink.

I'm a throwback, he says about the activator. I'm the futurepast. I'm one of those past perfect present niggas.

He looks dumber than anything I've seen and I've seen some superdumb shit.

Like my dad is pretty dumb. He pisses in two-liter Cherry Coke bottles cause he's too lazy to slide out of his wheelchair. He's put on about eighty pounds in the last year. He even started wearing diapers.

You think I'm changing you? I'll say.
I can do it, he'll answer.
I'm like, Big-ass baby.

I have to Febreze the whole house cause he stinks so bad. This social worker nurse used to come by but she got caught using someone else's Social Security Number and the government sent her back to Mexico. Her name was Lupe. She had a big flat ass and a mouth like a circus clown.

Get another nurse, I told my dad. Your disability pays for it.
I don't want another one, he whined. I want Lupe.
He won't call for another one.

I miss Lupe, he'll sometimes say.
I'll say, Stop crying, sissy. Just stop.

And then he'll take some Oxycotton or this stuff called Lortab and park his wheelchair in front of the TV and watch one of his reality shows and eat Breyers double chocolate ice cream right out of the carton.

Another superdumb thing:

There was this seventh grader who used to faint all the time. His name was Jason Salerno and in shop he was afraid of the electric saw.

It's just a saw, Mr. Gass told him. We won't even use that till next year.

But he would faint in every class. His body would collapse like a kiddie pool after you knife it. You could practically hear the air hissing out of his body.

Sometimes I would go up to Salerno in the hall and just say the word.

Saw, I would say. Saw.

He would start running to his next class.

Dumb.

About getting sucked off by a guy, I don't give a rat's ass. I just closed my eyes and pictured Bounce doing me.

Oh, Orange, she cried in my mind. Oh, Orange, you're so big and hard.

Lyde calls me Huck Finn and whimpers when he's doing me.

Huck, he'll wheeze. Motherfucking Huck.

For a big security guard he sure is a pussy. He works at Best

Buy so he can get Blu-ray DVD players and Canon products. He put the copy machine in a bag with a receipt and everything. So now we got posters of the Frog. Posters and flyers. Bounce brings good paper from her parents' home office. Her mom and dad are sales reps for Plaxco, this company that makes prescription pills. Apparently there's this new pill that lets you see the future. Bounce says she's going to get some so we can have psychic knowledge.

We started the Frog Collection about five weeks ago. Our system is tight. Wiggins is the watchdog and Bounce and me are the brains and muscle.

When we collect, Bounce does most of the talking cause she's got communication skills. She told me how in speech drama and journalism she always got the top grade and how she gave a speech about the human jaw, all the bones and hinges. How it can be broken and how you got to suck your food through a straw while it's healing. Bounce can talk about the difference between the human jaw and the horse jaw. She can talk about the alligator jaw and how it snaps.

Bounce's real name is Carla Reuschel, but if you call her Carla you better be ready to fight.

When we knock on doors I just stand there with the collection can. Bounce does a speech about the Frog and how we're taking donations to help find her.

What do the donations go to? they'll ask.

We make posters, Bounce'll say. Posters and flyers. We post her picture on bulletin boards all throughout the Dumas community. The YMCA, St. Jude's, the Library. We need to do something to find this poor girl. We use the Internet too.

The truth is we don't do shit on the Internet — we don't got a website or nothing — but in plop the quarters anyway.

Plop plop.

In slide the dollar bills.

Swish swish.

Even a twenty now and then.

Bounce'll say, Andrew Jackson, you pretty bitch.

Little do they know, little do they know.

We've been averaging about twelve bucks a day. One day we made eighty-five. Sometimes people invite us in and feed us. Like grilled cheeses and microwave burritos. If that happens I take their salt and pepper shakers. I keep them in a pillowcase in my room at home.

You're a good thief, Bounce will say.

I'm in love with her. We don't do nothing yet but sometimes she lets me put my hand on her beautiful round stomach.

Let me have some, I'll plead.
You beg like a dog, she'll say.

She don't care that Lyde does me.

It's for the greater good, she'll say. You're taking one for the team.
You're crewing for the crew.

Bounce

I know the good people of Dumas think I'm peculiar because my crew consists of a pair of poor, dirty, irresponsible, scholastically retarded, pubescently challenged seventh-grade loner chuckle-heads. Tom Toomer Junior High School is made up of rich kids and poor kids. There's not much in between. I happen to have been brought into this world by a set of parents who are super-naturally wealthy thanks to their accelerated ascent up the pharmaceutical conglomerate they both work for and now actually own shares of. I'm not supposed to take interest in the unlucky or the disposable members of my peer group. Then again, I'm not supposed to be doing most of the things I do.

We watched this film in advanced natural sciences featuring a herd of migrating wildebeests attempting to cross a river in the

Sudan. A congregation of crocodiles came heaving up out of the water and slaughtered a third of the herd. You could see the bodies of several wildebeests being severed in half by the deadly crocodile jaws. It was impressive to say the least. The biomechanics of it. Mr. Flint was teaching us about the brutality of natural selection and the instinct to survive.

I see Wiggins and Orange as two lost wildebeests — two of the unlucky ones — and I'm just trying to help them get to the other side of the river.

I'm their river guard.

Big momma River Guard.

I met the chuckleheads in detention.

The detention supervisor, Mrs. Slakeberry, had to use the washroom and put me in charge of the room because she was aware of my startlingly high grade-point average. Wiggins, Orange, and I were the only ones in detention that day. Wiggins was pretending to be studying his language arts textbook and Orange was slumped so low in his desk chair it was like he lost his ass in a car accident.

I'm in charge, I told them.

They didn't say anything in response because my commanding reputation obviously preceded me.

After a minute, I asked them, Do you know each other?
Orange said, I don't know that fag.

Wiggins wouldn't say anything, the stubborn little beauty. He was wearing a Chicago Bulls T-shirt and his big hazel eyes looked heavenly.

Why are you in detention? I asked him.
'Cause I missed the bus, Wiggins replied.

I asked him how he got to school and he told me he walked.

How far? I asked.
I don't know, he said. Far.
Where do you live?
He said, In a apartment.
I said, *An* apartment. Why'd you miss the bus?
He replied, 'Cause my mom forgot to wake me up.
Don't you have an alarm clock?
No, he said.
Here, I said, come here.

He walked over to me and I gave him my Timex Ironman Global Trainer GPS watch.

He took it and looked at it like it was the heart of a lion cub beating in his hand.

Don't be late anymore, I said.

He didn't even say thanks because he was too amazed.

Wiggins still wears the watch. He hates to get it dirty. I don't think he's ever taken it off.

Then I asked Orange why he was in detention and he said how he punched Sarah Margin after she narked on him for trying to copy her multiple-choice pop quiz about the French Revolution.

Let them eat cake, I said.
He had no idea what I was referring to and made a face like he'd swallowed a fork.
Eighteenth-century bullshit, I added. Where'd you punch her? I asked.
In the stomach, he replied
In class?
At the water fountain.
You like punching girls? I asked.
He said, I don't give a four-legged fuck. Girls. Little kids. Old people.
I said, What about animals?
I'd punch a cat, he answered.
He scratched his orange hair and dandruff floated onto his shoulders.

Why'd *you* get detention? Orange asked me.
Because I challenged Mr. Kantu to an arm-wrestling match.
No shit? he said.
Mr. Kantu? Wiggins chimed in. The football coach?
We were discussing derivatives in Advanced Calc, I explained. I raised my hand and challenged him.

Did he do it? Orange asked.

Nope, I said.

He's got big arms, Wiggins said.

I would've whipped him, I said.

How do you know? Orange asked.

I said, Because I know the secret.

What secret? Wiggins asked.

The secret to winning in arm wrestling.

What is it? Orange asked, the dummy.

Forearm strength, I answered.

Then to Orange I said, You wanna punch me?

No, he answered.

Come on, I said, punch me. It'll feel good. You can punch me right in the face.

Then Mrs. Slakeberry returned from the bathroom.

Thank you, Carla, she said.

She had brushed her hair and put it up in a bun.

Was everything okay? she asked.

Everything was great, I replied.

After detention I invited them to go to the mall with me.

My mom's picking me up in the Lexus, I told them.

Both their faces changed when they heard the word Lexus. Put a poor kid in a one-hundred-and-eleven-thousand-dollar car and watch him suddenly act polite. They were polite as pussy willows.

It's a six-hundred-h, I told them. Five-liter V-eight engine, continuously variable transmission, satellite radio, iPod input, DVD player. She'll drop us off, pick us up, drive us home, door-to-door service.

So that day after detention they came to the mall with me. We ate Cinnabons and played video games and went to a Mel Gibson movie.

That was back in January and we've been inseparable since.

They like me because I'm rich and maternal.

And I like them because they're lost and stupid.

One of them is also pretty but the other one is just lost and stupid.

The Frog

they come out of the trees
they walk slow and their eyes glow yellow
I can see them from far away
I am the best at seeing them
my arms are dirty from the mud and the bugs
last night they got dingdong and becky
dingdong was pushing becky up a tree but they got him from
behind and then becky fell and they got her too
becky was my friend
she talked about dolls and sparkles
they ate her head, the hair and everything
dingdong was dumb but he had a nice face and he told me about
his pet duck and his train set

when the wolves come I make myself skinny so they cant smell
me
they cant smell me and if I make myself skinny enough they
wont eat me cause they dont like it when its just bones
they like it if youre chubby or if you got big feet or a fat butt
theres another boy who can run fast
his name is shane and hes got a face like a catfish
shane caught a bird and we ate it with some sticks
shane ate a stick too which made him slow and stupider than
dingdong but he got smart again after the moon came
I am smaller than the others and I like my tree
raheem is chubby and he lets me curl up near his belly
he told me I would soon eat a wolf
soon he said
soon you will eat one and then more birds will come

toofairy feeds me and lets me tinkle and I know he is good

Wiggins

The Frog was on the news again.

Dirty Diana was watching it when I walked in. She was bleaching her feet and eating a big bag of Tostitos.

You sec this? she said. Poor little girl.

According to the news, the Frog's real name is Laurel May Gillett. This anchorwoman said she's three-and-a-half and that she's allergic to nuts. The anchorwoman's hair looked like it would taste like a birthday cake. Her name is Ronette Stone and she said the Frog's nut allergy is potentially fatal and they showed her preschool picture and talked about how the police had formed a special task force to find her, how they were going to use all these German shepherds.

The Dumas toddler has been missing for nearly ten weeks, Ronette Stone told all the viewers.

She talked about her parents Paul and Gina Gillett and her older brother Davey and her baby sister Birdy. Then they appeared all huddled on their living room sofa. There was a fireplace and a giant gray cat lying across the sofa with a face like a fat president.

Please bring our little girl back to us, Gina Gillett pleaded, crying to all the viewers. Please.

I miss my sister, Davey said. He wore big glasses and a White Sox hat and looked like one of those kids with a lot of birthmarks. Like he might have a big purple one on his stomach.

For some reason I imagined the Gilletts going sledding in the snow. Going sledding and then maybe drinking hot cocoa under a Christmas tree, one of those big white fake ones with a toy donkey and some upside-down angels under it. A paper star on top. I don't know why I imagined that cause it was hot as hell in the living room. It was like a hundred degrees and Dirty Diana was sweating and scratching her feet.

On TV Ronette Stone went, If you have any information or anonymous tips, please call the following number.

They showed the number on the screen.

Somebody better call that number! Dirty Diana yelled. What the fuck is wrong with everybody!

She turnt to me and went, You see this shit?!

She'd been drinking Bartles and Jaymes Melon Splashes. She'd had like three bottles and the living room stunk.

You're drunk, I told her.
No I'm not, she said.

Her mouth got all small and her chin started quivering and I thought she was going to cry.

I said, Take your drunk ass to bed, and then I went to my room and did so many push-ups I got cramps in my arms.

Before I fell asleep I couldn't stop thinking about the Frog's nut allergy.

* * *

The next day I told Bounce and Orange how the Frog was on the news. We were in Bounce's parents' Lexus, going to buy more cereal and milk for the Frog at Econofoods. Bounce was driving and Orange was in the passenger's seat. I was in the back like always.

I told them about the Frog and her parents and her brother and sister. And how she's allergic to nuts.

31

She's got some condition, I said. If she eats a nut she'll die.

She can eat *these* nuts, Orange said, grabbing his junk.

Her parents are really pale, I added. Their names are Paul and Gina.

I saw them on the news, Bounce said. Little Birdy looks like she got left in the broiler too long.

I was like, The police are starting a task force with German shepherds.

She said, It's about time, the geniuses.

Two days later Bounce got this human scent eliminator called the Oxy Elim-A-Scent. It kills human smells in areas up to fifty feet.

Hunters use this, she said. It basically makes them undetectable.

Bounce bought it off the Internet with her parents' credit card and had it FedExed overnight. It looks like a stereo speaker and takes four triple-A batteries.

We put it in Orange's basement, right over the washer-dryer unit.

Now we don't got to worry about no German shepherds.

Orange

I had this dream that my mom was trapped inside a vacuum cleaner. The vacuum cleaner was in the middle of this dirty field full of broken beer bottles and rusted-out cars and half-burnt picnic tables. I was walking through the field when I heard my mom's voice.

Timothy! she cried. In here, Timothy!

I tried to open the back of the vacuum cleaner, but it wouldn't budge. I found a rock and hit it like a thousand times. I even used a car part. Then I realized the vacuum cleaner was plugged into this huge telephone pole so I turnt it on cause I thought that would somehow make it open, but the vacuum cleaner started sucking up all the broken glass and car parts from the field.

It was vibrating like crazy and blood was suddenly spilling out of it.

I could hear my mom screaming, so I turnt it off.

I was like, Mom? . . . Mom?

But all you could hear was her screaming.

Now whenever I see a vacuum cleaner I feel like my head might pop off.

Even a DustBuster fucks me up.

I threw our vacuum cleaner out two days ago. It was in the broom closet next to this life-size cardboard cutout of Paula Abdul from American Idol. My dad was sitting in the living room, watching The Ghost Whisperer and he barely noticed. I think he used to sleep with it. I heard him talking to it once.

Oh, Paula, he said. Come on now, Paula.

I didn't just leave the vaccuum in front of the house. I walked it all the way down the street and put it in the dumpster.

I hate dreams.

Dreams and tunafish.

Bounce

The whole thing with the Frog started with the Poet, Wilbur Logg. He came and spoke to Honors English. We'd been reading *Animal Farm* and Mr. Moyer said he had a surprise for us, that some famous poet who lived nearby was kind enough to take time out of his busy schedule to visit class and that we would resume our George Orwell discussion next time.

So this tall man with gray hair walks in. He's wearing jeans and a white button-down shirt and beat-up tennis sneakers from the seventies. He's pretty old, like sixty-something, and he isn't moving too great — he has to use a cane.

Sorry about the limp, he said. I'm afraid arthritis doesn't discriminate.

There were only twelve of us in Honors English and none of us had ever met a professional writer before. Earlier that semester, as an assignment we had to write a letter to our favorite living author, and some of us got responses, but no one had actually seen a professional writer in the flesh.

I wrote to this guy named J.T. Clarke, not because I like his books, but because he looks pathetic.

> Dear Mr. Clarke, I wrote.
>
> Your author photo makes you look like you often fall prey to your own physical ineptitude. Do you always wear those glasses, or did you put them on for the photo to intentionally look less masculine?
>
> Sincerely,
>
> Carla Reuschel
> Honors English
> Tom Toomer Junior High School

Personally I think books are useless and I told Wilbur Logg as much.

This is how that started:

How many of you enjoy reading? he asked.

His big sad poet eyes. His thinning gray poet hair.

Of course, Sophia George raised her delicate little hand. Wilbur Logg asked her what her favorite books were and she started listing all the so-called great ones, like *The House of Mirth* and *Lord of the Flies* and *The Old Man and the Sea*.

Then Cory Bath said something about *The Great Gatsby* and how it still relates to the world today and I must've made a hate face because Wilbur Logg looked straight at me and said, And what's your name?

That's Carla, Mr. Moyer said. Carla Rueschel. One of our best and brightest.

Wilbur Logg said, What books do you like, Carla?

I said, I don't.

Oh, he said. You're in Honors English and you don't read?

No, I read, I said. I just don't like books.

He said, And why's that?

I said, Because they bore me, kid.

Everyone was pretty shocked I called him kid.

Wilbur Logg said, I'm sorry you feel that way, Carla.

Bounce, I said.

Mr. Moyer took his glasses off and made a pained face.

Wilbur Logg rubbed his bushy gray poet eyebrows and said, I personally think books are one of the greatest things about being alive. Novels. Plays. Volumes of poetry.

I said, But a book doesn't really change anything. It's just a lot of words.

And the Poet said, I think a book can *absolutely* change things.

Like what? I said. Your grade from a B to an A?

He said, Literature can inspire revolution. Words are absorbed purely by the reader. The reader creates the world of the story with the author. He or she is in essence a performer. It's an experience that can excite all the senses.

I said, Not in my opinion, Wilbur.

Carla, Mr. Moyer said, come on now.

I said, Thinking's not doing.

But thinking can lead to doing, Wilbur Logg said.

Doing's doing, I said. I'm a doer.

Then Wilbur Logg turned to Mr. Moyer and said, Mr. Moyer, is Carla always this tough?

Mr. Moyer said, She can certainly be challenging but she's one of our finest.

I said, Don't talk about me like I'm not here, Arthur. And watch your adverb placement.

Carla, Mr. Moyer said. Don't be disrespectful, please.

Then I recited Mr. Moyer's mailing address just to keep him off balance.

I said, Arthur Moyer: Three-fifty-two West Street, apartment seven.

That sure as shit shut him up, the chucklehead.

After a silence during which I ate half of a Heath bar, Wilbur Logg said, I'm sorry you feel that way about books, Carla.

I said, It's Bounce, you slug.
He said, Excuse me?
Nothing, I said. Don't mind me.

Sophia George wanted my Heath bar. I know the anorexic vegan wanted it more than anything.

Wilbur Logg said, I'm sorry you feel that way about books, Bounce. Hopefully someday you'll read one that will change your mind.
Not likely, I said.
And he said, Well, you're missing out on one of life's great joys.
I offered, You sort of already said that, sporto.

That got a laugh too.

Then he opened a small paperback book with a goat on a mountain called *The Goat on the Mountain and Other Poems* and he read us a poem about drinking black coffee and some pears on a table. Utter useless bullshit. While he was reciting the poem he made a face like God was whispering in his ear.

After he was finished Mr. Moyer led an applause and then Wilbur Logg closed his book and said, Does anyone here understand the meaning of capitalism?

No one answered. You could hear the light buzzing over us. I love that sound. It means school isn't working, that the teachers are losing the battle.

39

He said, I realize you're only in the eighth grade, but I understand you're all quite advanced.

Sophia George raised her hand. Sophia George with her big brown eyes and her delicate hands. Her ass the size of a cantaloupe. She plays the piano and she's never late for class. I'm going to put an end to her piano playing. I have a plan that involves a popular carpentry tool used for driving nails.

Wilbur Logg called on her and Sophia George said, Free-market economy.
Good, he said. Very good. Anyone else?
Skip McKee said, The opposite of Iraq.
And what is their economic system? Wilbur Logg asked.
Iraqi, I said, and everyone laughed.
Some of them laughed because they were scared but Todd Bender thought it was genuinely funny. You could tell by the way he put his hand over his mouth all discreet.

Then Wilbur Logg went on to talk about how our country is greedy and how everyone wants *more more more* and how everything is bloated and supersized and how all our food is pumped full of chemicals and hormones and how our bloodstreams are clogged with cholesterol and how, even though presumably we live in a free-market economy and dance to the narcotic choruses of let freedom ring and the egalitarian dictates of a people-be-heard democracy that all of this grotesque consumerism limits our freedom. He said it isn't our fault — meaning the twelve eighth graders in Mr. Moyer's Honors English class — that we are owned by these false systems, but that the fault lies with the older

40

generations and the fault lies with television and the fault lies with Sears catalogs and the fault lies with the Internet and the fault lies with the media and Fox News in particular and on and on and on like that.

He was so filled with passion, I thought his neck would burst. I could almost see blood splattered on the chalkboard.

There was a long pause during which he caught his breath and wiped his forehead with a handkerchief.

You could hear the lights buzzing over us again.

You all are in prison, he added somberly. You don't realize it, children, but you're in prison.

I ain't no chile, I said.

I said it like a nigger, and Todd Bender laughed again.

Then in my regular voice I said, If I'm in prison, I'm having a pretty good time.

Wilbur Logg took a breath and said, Bounce, may I ask what it is that you do for a good time?
I answered, Why, you looking for a good time?
He said, I'm talking about extracurricular activities.
I said, I watch TV. I play video games. I go to the mall. I eat Cinnabons and Sbarro pizza.
He said, And what are you passionate about?

Extreme fighting, I answered. Especially cage matches. The hard-core jams. Bare-knuckle battles. Stuff you can't even see on pay-per-view.

Where might one see this sort of thing? he asked.

On the Internet, I said. And I supersize my combo meal every time I go to Mickey Dees.

He shook his head and said, God help you.

And that's when he sealed his fate.

God help me.

I said, God has a cotton-ball beard and werewolf hair.

I said, God's too busy conducting conference calls with Santa Claus and the Easter Bunny.

That's enough, Carla! Mr. Moyer said, his glasses off again. No more!

I just smiled and ate the rest of my Heath bar.

And that night I decided to kidnap the Frog. Sometimes it takes the smallest thing to start an important, irreversible chain of events. I'd been seeing her by the Home Depot. That's where I go get my Slurpees and throw rocks at the old man who breaks down boxes in back of the 7-Eleven. I never hit him—I miss him on purpose. I just like watching the foolio jump.

The way I explained it to my crew was like this:

We were in the cafeteria, eating chicken-cutlet sandwiches.

Orange, I said, Wiggins, we're about to change the world.

I told them about how we would kidnap the Frog and then when the time was right, we'd start collecting money on her behalf. And how we would use the money to make a famous poet disappear.

What's wrong with the Poet? Wiggins asked, hot-lunch crumbs all over his Salvation Army T-shirt.
He takes up the wrong kind of space, I answered. There's the right kind of space and the wrong kind of space. It's as simple as that.

And that seemed to satisfy him.

To Wiggins I said, You trust me, right?

Wiggins nodded.

You too, Firebox.

Orange also nodded, the chucklehead.

They were in like Flynn.

I said, My perfect little monkey boys.

Orange, with his long stupid face and his curly red hair, and little Wiggins, with his hazel cat eyes and long pretty lashes and his old man walk and the knife he keeps in his pocket like a promise.

Three is a magic number.

A prefect triangle.

An unholy trinity.

The Frog

theres a monster crying upstairs
I think hes a good monster cause his crying has a song in it
sometimes I can hear him breathing in the floor

I wanna give him a hamburger
a hamburger and a flower and a cupcake with blue sprinkles

Wiggins

His house is a old red barn.

Bounce got the address cause her English class had to write to him after he visited. His barn house is outside of Dumas, off of Frontage Road, where the cornfields turn into dirty black hills.

When we pulled up to the Poet's barn house I looked in the window expecting to see some cows or sheep or a huge horse attached to a tractor or like a big white windmill with some pigs under it but it was just him and he was rocking back and forth in a rocking chair and smoking a pipe.

Bounce dropped me off and was like, Be a good monkey-scout. Efficiency wins the war.

I knew I had to scout good and fast cause I had to walk home and it was already starting to get dark.

I knocked on the door to see if he had a dog. There was a big black one with yellow eyes and it barked with viciousness. It was too big for me to fight. I figured it could kill me before I could stab it. I ain't afraid to stab no dog, it's just risky, specially cause black dogs like to bite white people, cause dogs is racist just like everyone else.

After I saw its yellow eyes I ran back to the road and jogged home.

It was so dark I started to get nervous about UFOs. But sort of excited too. There wasn't no cars and the corn was breathing. I had to stop jogging cause my lungs were burning. I puked in the gravel and then I had to sit down for a minute. The crickets and the corn and the mystery bugs and the heat was like hypnotism on my mind. I was sweating like a fat church nigger. I could smell my own stink coming through my clothes. Sometimes I think my stink makes me want to commit crimes against people and against societies. Legendary crimes like burning down houses or making mass murders or robbing that place where they keep all the gold in Fort Knocks. There's a good stink and a bad stink. Mine is mostly bad.

The moon was sick and gray like it had a fungus. It kept disappearing behind the clouds and it seemed like it was losing power. Like it might fall a thousand feet and turn into space slobber.

When I got home, Dirty Diana was asleep in her nurse's uniform.

It looked more like a costume than a uniform. Like she got drunk and passed out at a Halloween party.

Before I fell asleep I couldn't stop picturing myself fighting the Poet's big black dog. Like a real hellified fight to the death. I would stab him but he would keep coming at me with his yellow eyes. Like he couldn't be killed no matter how many times you stabbed him.

* * *

The next day we were at the Mickey Dees on Bantum Boulevard, eating Extra Value Meals. I was supersizing like a fiend.

He's got a dog, I reported. Big black dog.
Bounce was like, So we'll poison it.
I went, Poison it how?
We'll put the poison in some Alpo burgers. Throw them in his backyard.
Orange said, Bye-bye, Fido.

So then me and Orange had to go to this guy's place on Locke Street. His name is Tab and his house was half-broken down like there were some walls missing and you could see the wires and the pipes in the ceiling and there was a mound of dirt in the kitchen. The whole place smelled like wet paint and cat piss.

Tab is old — like at least fifty-something — with a brown wig and a brown mustache and yellow stains under his eyes. His homo roommate Neal went to get the poison. Neal is only a couple of years older than Orange and me. He has long hippie hair and he wears bright red lipstick.

When Neal came back with the poison I said, Are you like sposed to be a clown?
He smiled and went, Do you like clowns?

He handed Orange a brown bag with the bottle of poison in it.

I pointed to the mound of dirt and said, What's that for?
Flowers, Tab answered. Do you like flowers?
I was like, No.
Neal said, We're starting a vegetable garden.
I said, In your kitchen?
Tab said, Is *that* what you think this room is? One man's kitchen is another man's vegetable garden.

Then Neal asked us if we wanted tea.

He said, Tea, boys?
Orange was like, We gotta go.

Tab was wearing a fuzzy blue bathrobe and slippers. His mustache had yellow in it, which matched the stains under his eyes.

I noticed that part of a ladder was laid over where some of the staircase was missing. Somewhere in the house a baby was crying. It might have been on a TV but I think it was real. It was either a baby or a cat getting heated.

Then Orange crumpled the bag of poison. He was scared, I could see it in his eyes. He nudged me and then I paid him for the poison and we backed out of the crazy house.

* * *

That night we soaked the Alpo burgers in a pan of the poison and put them in a big Ziploc bag and then Bounce drove me to the Poet's red barn in the Lexus. I walked around to the back, near this little shed.

Through a window in the shed I could see the Poet writing at a desk. There was a spiral notebook in front of him and he was making a face like he was praying. His desk was made out of a door and there was stacks of books and jars of pens all over it. There was a coffee machine and a clock radio too. His big black dog was sleeping in a blanket on the floor.

I was starting to roll on some Oxycotton Bounce gave me when we soaked the Alpo burgers. She likes giving me Oxycotton. The other day she gave me some Speed Stick deodorant too.

The crickets sounded like Coke bottles sliding on a icy street. Even though it was hot as fuck I was thinking about ice and winter and a big snowman holding a Domino's pizza. Like the delivery man got froze in a blizzard.

I think I got too close to the window cause I could see my breath steaming on the glass.

This man don't got nothing, I thought. Just a dog and some books and a coffee machine.

For a second I felt myself passing through the glass, like I was a ghost or like I was the sound of those crickets. My one knee wobbled and I had to keep myself from falling. Sometimes my knee falls asleep and I have to punch it.

Instead of planting the Alpo burgers in the backyard I threw the Ziploc bag on the roof of the shed.

On the way home I said, That man don't got nothing.
Bounce was like, Poets don't *want* anything.
I said, How come?
Bounce went, Because they think they're above it all. They look down on us consumers.
I was like, What's a consumer?
And Bounce said, An American. A happy American.
Then I said, It was just him and his dog.
She said, Poets don't know what real living is.
I said, You think he's got a family?

Bounce turnt to me and said, You feel sorry for him.

I flipped on the air-conditioner and she flipped it off and went, Don't feel sorry for that old chucklehead.
I don't, I said. I don't.
Then Bounce told me I was too sensitive.
I was like, No I ain't.

Then we drove some more and she went, You planted the Alpo burgers, right?

Of course, I answered.

Lying to Bounce made me feel all loose inside. Like my stomach was a sponge full of sewer water.

Bounce said, It's what he *represents* that matters, Wiggins.

What does he represent? I asked.

She said, He takes the fucking un out of fun. The sin out of Cinnabon. Life's too short for that, right?

I nodded and then she turnt the headlights off and it was so dark it was like we were nowhere. I could feel a thrill in my nuts and stomach. You could almost hear all the houses whispering to each other.

Look at those freaks, they told each other. Look at those nobody kids.

The crickets and the houses and the clouds slipping around in the sky.

I said, What would your parents do if they found out you was driving their car?

She said, They wouldn't do shit.

I was like, But you're only fourteen.

She said, Wiggins, Dapper Dan and Kara have nine-volt batteries in their backs. All I have to do is change the batteries now and then. Besides, they're always gone on business. Selling happy pills

to all the sad people. They don't know shit about me.
I said, But you don't got no license. What if you got caught?
Bounce was like, They're the ones who would get in trouble.
I went, Why?
She said, Because I'm their fucking daughter. Their legal ward.
I was like, But you would get busted, too, ain't it?
Bounce went, You think I'm afraid of getting busted?

And then she turnt the headlights back on.

We drove past the mall. It was all lit up and perfect. We stopped at
a traffic light. In the parking lot there was all these people getting
in their cars. I saw this man and his wife with their little kid. They
were all holding hands, walking to their big silver SUV. I wanted
to go take the kid. He was pretty small and wearing a Cardinals
baseball hat. I would put him in the basement with the Frog and
call him Toad. They would wash each other and tell each other
stories. Maybe they would fight each other too. And then fall in
love. After a while, maybe I could find them a lizard or make them
a ant farm.

Before Bounce dropped me off in front of my apartment building
I said, So are we gonna feed those Alpo burgers to the Frog, too?
She said, You want to, huh?

I didn't answer.

Part of me wanted to feed her the Alpo burgers and part of me
didn't. The Frog is really confusing like that.

Before I got out Bounce kissed me on the cheek.

She said, Hey, big eyes.
I said, Hey.
She went, You're a good little monkey.
I went, Thanks.
Bounce put her forehead on mine and said, We love each other, right?

I nodded.

I pictured love as a big hairy giant with a dead fish in his mouth. Grizzly bear claws and his heart half out of his chest cause it's too big and the lungs have to fit. He never stops walking. Over mountains. Through the desert. On top of icy lakes. Past huge cities. And he hunts and kills for you and always comes back with plenty to eat.

Her kiss was cold on my skin.

This is all going to be amazing, she said. You'll see.

Then she put another Oxycotton in my mouth. The other one was still going strong, but two is better than one.

Orange always says, Twice as nice for a very low price.

I walked around the apartment complex. It was like I was a fugitive with bullets in my back. Or like I got Tasered by a security guard at the mall.

I wanted the new Oxycotton to kick in before I went home.

Hurry up, I told the Oxycotton. Hurry the fuck up.

Mosquitoes were infesting the light in front of my building. I looked up at our living room window. It's on the third floor and faces the street. I could see how the screen was missing, just like the one in Dirty Diana's room. I wondered why it couldn't never get fixed right. Maybe Mr. Song or his mute wife come and ruin it no matter how many times it gets replaced. Like in the middle of the night when everyone's asleep. Management will keep you down. They're sneaky and they're always adding late fees to your rent. Late fees and other fees for maintenance. Dirty Diana calls Mr. Song Charlie Chinco.

She says, Charlie Chinco and his snap-on haircut.

That shit does look snap-on, Orange said when Mr. Song was fixing our garbage disposal.

Let's pull it off, he whispered.

In the parking lot someone had painted the tops of the dumpsters black and you could smell the paint cutting through the hot air. The stars were blasting so bright it was like they had emotions. Like they were rolling too.

I thought about space and how quiet it must be up there. So quiet and nothing stupid going on. No bugs or shitty smells. Just stars and planets and a floaty feeling. Sometimes I wish they would come and get me. They meaning them creatures from Mr. Merlo's alien abduction books. I would let them have me naked. My nuts and everything. I would step right out of my clothes and board their ship and let them stick me with space pins and turn me into their earthling ho.

The Oxycotton was starting to kick in. My whole body felt like it was smiling.

Hello, Piano Road, I said, laughing. Hello.

* * *

At home Dirty Diana was on her cell phone. I think she was talking to this big Mexican called Cortina. Cortina's a security guard at the casino boat over in Rockwood. The casino boat's on the Wall River. They met cause his kid Paco died from a car crash. Dirty Diana was Paco's nurse—when they had him hooked up to machines—and she saw Cortina crying at his son's bedside and she felt sorry for his immigrant ass. Cortina was driving and his wife died from the crash too. They didn't bother hooking her up to no machines cause her head got knocked off. Sometimes when he comes over him and Dirty Diana sit on the couch together but they don't even hold hands.

Sometimes I just want to say, At least hug her. If you ain't gonna fuck her at least hug her!

Once he let me hold his security guard badge.

You want it? he asked.

It felt fake in my hand so I gave it back.

How come you don't got a gun? I asked.
He said, Cause I ain't no cop. I got a billyclub.
I said, Where is it?
At the job, he answered. I leave it in my locker.

Part of me wanted to show Dirty Diana the space where my tooth was cause I'd been keeping my mouth closed around her. I thought maybe they could put it back on at the hospital. Like they would give her a employee discount. I heard about how you can sew a finger back on if you soak it in milk first. I was ready to show her but she was turnt away.

Mom, I said. Mom.

But she waved me off.

In my room I opened the window and stared up at the stars again.

Come on, I said to them. Just come already.

I waited for Dirty Diana to finish watching Craig Ferguson and then I snuck out.

When I went to go feed the Frog she was standing on the other side of the TV.

What's wrong? I said.

The bike chain was pulled tight and her whole body was frozen.

There's a woof down here, she said.
Where? I asked. Where?
She was like, In the fridgeranor.

I went over and opened the Merlos' old fridge. There was this big
hole torn in the back of it. Inside was a dead raccoon. It stunk like
pure badness. When I lifted it up by the tail there were dead baby
raccoons underneath it. They looked blind and slimy. I put the
raccoon and her babies in a old pillowcase that was stuck behind
the washer-dryer unit.

Dead coon, I said to the Frog.
She was like, Can I see?

I opened the pillowcase and showed her.

She said, Coombabies.

I nodded.

You gonna bury 'em? She asked.
Yeah, I lied.
When? she asked.
Right now, I said.
She said, Can I come?

She tugged on the bike chain and I shook my head.

She went, Okay, and then started the video game. She had gotten really far on it. The wolves were really skinny and tired. I watched her send a child down from the trees and bop one on the head with a rock. Then the child used the rock to saw the wolf's head off and then she brought five other children down from the trees and they ate the wolf clean to its spine. Then they laughed and burped and helped each other climb back up the trees.

You're getting good, I told her.

But I don't think she could hear me. Her eyes were huge and she wasn't blinking.

I brought the pillowcase up from the basement and threw it outside in the trash.

When I came back in, Mr. Merlo was in the hallway, sitting on the floor with his legs straight out, slumped against the wall. He wasn't wearing no shirt. He's got big hairy breasts and a obesity stomach.

Wiggins, he said.
I said, Hey, Mr. Merlo.
Wiggins, Wiggins, Wiggins.

It seemed like he was having trouble breathing.

I was like, Where's your wheelchair?

In the living room, he said.

Why are you on the floor? I asked.

He said, Because I was seeing if I could walk.

He was making this weird growling noise and he was saying his words with a lot of carefulness. He was smiling too and his eyes were bugging.

He said, Some summer, eh?

I said, Should I call somebody?

No, he said. No need for that. I'm just resting.

I was like, Do you want me to go get your chair for you?

I'll make my way back to it, he said. I can use the exercise. After all, it's the summer. Time to go the beach.

His legs looked all skinny and white and dead. There wasn't no hair on them. It was like they were made of candy.

He said, What's going on down there in the basement?

I was like, There was a raccoon in the fridge.

He went, A coon. You don't say?

It was dead, I said. Don't worry, I cleaned everything up.

Animals, he said. Gotta love animals.

The he growled more and smiled and frowned at the same time. His chin was really buried in his chest. I couldn't tell what was his beard and what was his chest hair.

He said, You're a good kid, Wiggins.

I nodded even though I know it's not true. I know I'm dirty thieving scum.

He said, You know that, right?

I nodded again.

He was like, There aren't many good ones left.

I just kept nodding.

Then I said, In all them alien abduction books, do they ever take kids?
Sometimes, he answered. They'll take just about anybody.
I went, But what about kids like me?
He said, I'm sure they'd love to have you, Wiggins.
I was like, Cool. Cool.
Then he said, I need you to do me a favor.
I said, What?
He said, Go get some diapers for me.
I said, From in your room?
No, he said. I need you to go to the store. I ran out.
It's pretty late, I said.
He went, It's barely midnight.
I said, What's open?
Econofoods is twenty-four hours, he said.
I was like, What about Orange?
He said, Tim doesn't concern himself with my issues.
I said, Yes he does.

He said, You can take the car. It hasn't been driven in a while but there's gas in it.

I said, I don't got a license.

He went, You don't?

I shook my head.

I'm only thirteen, I said.

Okay, he said. Okay.

Then he almost fell asleep.

When his eyes opened he said, What the heck, go ahead and take the car anyway. You're pretty coordinated, right?

I went, I'm coordinated.

He said, Driving's a piece of cake. I'll let you keep the change.

I thought about his Taurus. It's gray with rust spots. In a flash I saw me and the Frog driving off somewhere. I would take her to a amusement park and we'd ride one of those rollercoasters that twists upside-down and I'd get her a hotdog and some cotton candy.

Orange came down from upstairs. He just appeared like a spirit.

To Mr. Merlo he said, Where's your chair, fucko?

I said, He was trying to walk.

Orange was like, That'll be the day.

I'm going to walk, Mr. Merlo said.

To his dad Orange said, You quit rehab after two days!

Because I wasn't ready, he cried.

Mr. Merlo's eyes were really bulging now. Like he was trying to use them to breathe.

Jesus, Orange said. At least put a shirt on.
You put a shirt on! Mr. Merlo yelled back.

I went back down into the basement and washed my hands and fed the Frog a bowl of Chex and gave her her Flintstones multi-vitamin with extra C. I sat on the floor with her and watched her eat.

She said, Thanks, Toofairy.

She stopped eating her Chex for a second and touched my face.

What? I said. What's wrong?

Your toof, she said. What happened?
I got punched, I told her.

She was like, By who?
Doesn't matter, I said.
She said, Does it hurt?

I shook my head cause the truth was I was rolling double and nothing hurt. I could've got hit by a bus and I wouldn't have knowed the difference.

I would get her a hotdog and some cotton candy and then we'd go into the funhouse and stand in front of one of those big freaky mirrors and make faces.

She went, Where is it?

I reached into my pocket and gave her my tooth.

She said, I can have it?

I nodded. It looked big in her hand.

She said, Looks like a aminal toof.
I am a animal, I told her.
Are you a woof? She asked.
I'm a boy, I told her. Boys are animals. So are girls. You're part animal too.

It's good to tell little kids the truth about shit.

She said, I'm a aminal too?
I was like, That's right.
I'm a woof, she said.
You're a wolfgirl, I said.

I pointed to my tooth and said, Don't lose it or I'll punish you.

She nodded and started eating again. Her hair smelt. It was pretty, the way blond hair can be on a girl, but it stank like those dead raccoon babies. The whole basement smelt like that.

After she ate her vitamin she showed me her tongue and said, Do you love those dead aminal babies?

Her space alien eyes looked big and stupid.

I nodded and she kept eating.

She said, Do you love those dead aminal babies more than me?

I shook my head.

You could hear Orange arguing with Mr. Merlo. I think they were still in the hall. At some point Mr. Merlo started crying. He sounded like a car honking on the highway. It was like he was pressing a button to make the sound.

For a second I thought maybe him and Dirty Diana should move in together. She could come live at his place and help him change his diapers and borrow his car cause Dirty Diana crashed our Nissan Versa in March. Cortina could come over and Miggy too and they could all watch Skinemax and take Mr. Merlo's pain pills and maybe have a orgy.

You could hear how Orange went and got him his wheelchair and was helping his dad into it.

Mr. Merlo was grunting and groaning.

Stop crying, I heard Orange say. I'll go get you your goddamn diapers.

Orange

During the last week of school Bounce made Wiggins and me slap-box in the boys' bathroom. He was sposed to be in Language Arts and I was sposed to be in P.E. but Bounce put notes in our lockers.

Three rounds, Bounce said. Don't be pussies. Ninety seconds per round.

She uses the stopwatch feature on her iPhone 4.

Demarcus Peeples came in to take a piss but he turnt right around when he saw Bounce.

Come here, Peeples, she ordered.

But he didn't come in far enough to where I could grab him. He was lucky.

I'm taller than Wiggins and I got longer arms, but he's quick like a project nigger cause he lives in the nigger projects. He knows how to bob and weave and come up under you. He stuck me four times in the first round and I kept missing him. I caught his shoulder once but Bounce says that don't count.

Come on, Orange, she said. Hit that little pretty freak.

I was trying, I really was, but I kept missing.

Once I slapped the corner of the stall and cut my palm.

In the second round I caught Wiggins on the top of the head, but that don't count as much as a slap to the eye or mouth. Bounce keeps points in her head.

Twelve-eight Wiggins, she said.

After I grazed his jaw, Wiggins came up under me again and popped my chin and I bit my tongue and it started bleeding.

Nice, Wiggins, Bounce said. Good little beast!

I could taste the blood in my mouth. Blood tastes stupid like a doorknob.

During the third round we were both winded. I get tired cause I smoke too much weed with Lyde and his boy Starnell. Starnell's always got Jamaican skunk. So does this guy called Grover Cleveland Steamer who sprays down shoes at the bowling alley. He trades me dimebags for my dad's pain pills.

Wiggins don't smoke weed, and he's always doing push-ups so he's got fitness.

My best move was when I pushed Wiggins in the last stall and he fell back on the toilet and I smacked him good across the face. Then I got him with the left, and the right again. Pink snot was coming out his nose.

Fifteen-thirteen Wiggins, Bounce called, but I knew I was beating him and she was just trying to motivate her man.

Wiggins couldn't get off the toilet so I knew I had him.

When Bounce calls knuckles we get to use our fists. She only calls it for the last ten seconds.

Knuckles! she shouted.

Wiggins caught me square under my chin and got back to his feet. I hit him in his ear and then he caught me under the chin again and I bit my tongue even harder. Little fucker, I thought. Little quick white nigger bitch. I punched him square in the mouth as hard as I could and then it was over.

When we came out of the stall Bounce said, Good little monkey-boys. Good.

My fist hurt and my tongue was burning.

Wiggins spit a tooth into his hand. It was the one next to the two in the front.

And since the last week of school he's been walking around looking like one of those homeless kids from the halfway house over on Anthony Avenue. They're all either missing teeth or they got cigarette burns on their arms.

Who won? I asked.
It was a tie, Bounce said. Twenty-one to twenty-one.

I told Wiggins I was sorry for knocking his tooth out.
Fuck it, he said. It's just a tooth.
Bounce said, That's your eyetooth. You look tough. Now hug.

First I had to puke some blood in the sink and then we hugged.

Wiggins hugged me harder than I hugged him cause he's soft like that.

You smell like shit, I told him. Why don't you shower?
I shower, he said.

You both stink, Bounce said. Let's get out of here.

We snuck out in the cafeteria. The janitor sweeping the floor watched us walk through the tornado doors like it was nothing. His name is Barney and he used to be in prison for credit card scams but now he carries the Bible around in his back pocket and blesses everyone.

Bless you, he said as we were leaving. I think he even made the sign of the cross. People find Jesus and they get stupid as shit.

We walked over to Bounce's crib in Golden Oaks where the houses are so big you can grow trees in them. Her parents ain't never home. I've only seen them once. They both wear expensive clothes and they look like twins. It doesn't seem like Bounce is their daughter. Once I asked her if she was adopted.

I was like, Were you adopted?
She said, I came from nowhere.
I said, Are your parents really your parents?
I actually gave birth to *them*, she answered. They ran out of me with nice haircuts and Armani suits and went right to work for Plaxco. It was either pharmaceuticals or porn.

Then she gave us a Oxycotton each.

Meds for the Chuckleheads, she said.

Everything in her living room feels like it's from a museum. There's this chair that looks more like a statue than a chair. And a huge painting of a orange blob.

70

That's a Rothko, she said about the painting. It's worth almost as much as this house.

Then she told us how Rothko was a abstract expressionist and how he killed himself by slicing his arm open.

Wiggins went, What's abscratch express? Is that like a rap group?
Abstract expressionism is a school of painting, Bounce explained. It's a bunch of freeform sloppy bullshit that a few of them got famous for.
I said, I could've made that painting with a dead cat dipped in ice cream.
And Bounce was like, *You're* a dead cat dipped in ice cream.

Then she licked her finger and put it in my ear.

Their couch is so nice it's like you need a permission slip to sit on it.

Wiggins was really into the painting. He was staring up at it with his mouth open.

It's a headless buffalo, he said. You can see the little hairs on its back.
I was like, *You're* a headless buffalo, freak.

Showers, Bounce ordered.

We all went upstairs to her parents' bathroom and took a shower.

The bathroom was bigger than my bedroom. The bar of soap was green and smelt like salad dressing. The shampoo had a French name.

Bounce made us all take our clothes off on the count of three. I don't never wear no underwear so I was naked first. Bounce was second. And Wiggins wears underwear and basketball shorts under his jeans so it took him the longest.

I was like, Why you wear basketball shorts under your jeans?
And he said, Cause your mom likes the way they make my junk look.

He thinks he can get to me when he says shit about my mom like that but I could give two wild fucks about her.

Wiggins don't got pubes yet. At least I got like seven.

Bald bitches, Bounce said. Who's bigger?

I am, I said.

Go dick-to-dick, Bounce ordered, but Wiggins turnt towards the corner.

Wiggins is bigger, Bounce said. Bigger by a longshot.

She was just saying that, though, cause my junk is healthy.

Bounce's bush is black. She let me soap it up and I got a boner and then so did Wiggins.

Faggit, I said to him.
I ain't no faggit, he said back.

Focus, monkey-boys, she said. Focus.

After the shower, we all put big fluffy robes on. We were definitely starting to roll. Bounce gave Wiggins a extra Oxycotton for his tooth. Sometimes my dad'll take two of them pills and just stare out the patio doors and drink Cherry Coke and fart continuously. Bounce's parents got like whole bins of the shit. Oxycotton, muscle relaxers, and this stuff called Klonopin, which she says is for seizures and panic attacks.

Bounce fed us microwaved Cinnabons and we sat on the big gray couch and she showed us all these brochures of the prep schools her parents want to send her to. One is called the Kent School and it's in Connecticut, way out east. The buildings look perfect, like they got baked in a oven with some brownies.

My heart suddenly felt like there was a hook in it.

I imagined Bounce walking in between those buildings with a bunch of rich kids, wearing a uniform and kicking leaves and watching videos on their iPhones.

There was another school called Groton. And one called Canterbury.

I was like, We de-Frog her, right?

De-Frog the fucking Frog! Bounce laughed. How amazing would that be!

Poetic! I cried. Ribbit-ribbit!

Later we ate a Tombstone pizza and two more Cinnabons each.

Wiggins looked confused about stuff.

I was like, What's wrong with you?

Nothing, he said.

You look confused, I told him.

He said, You look like a ass-fuck.

I just laughed cause even though Wiggins finally took a shower he still looked funny with his tooth missing.

Bounce

The Kent School Admissions Essay Question (250–300 words):
With regard to being an individual, what do you feel most distinguishes you from your peers?

Say a girl sees a bird. A small blackbird. Say it appears to be dead.
Like it flew into a large bay window, mistakenly thinking it was
flying into a new vector of sky, fooled by the reflection. Or maybe
its heart broke because it saw something shift in nature. Like its
mother being mauled by a fox. Or maybe it was shot out of a tree
by a boy with a pellet gun. Say this girl encounters the fallen bird,
still alive, and wants to know more about its internal systems. So
she takes a tool to it — a hammer or a screwdriver — and pries it
open. Not out of cruelty or hatred, but out of a pure curiosity as

to how it's made. As to how it's different from other animals she has come to know. Its various connective tissues and the makings of its heart.

This girl pushes nature to an uncomfortable limit because she is not satisfied with what she is shown in school, on TV, on the Internet. Cheerleaders bore her. Varsity-letter winners are an absurd menagerie of cardboard joke people. She wants to know the shapes and odors of the world. She wants to get down in the dirt with the worms and the beetles. She wants to know the way meat moves through the packaging house. The way the animal body contains liquids and solids. The way muscle attaches to tendon. Ligaments. She wants to know these things from the smells she acquires on her hands.

She is not afraid of seismic discomfort.

She is not afraid of malice or beauty.

She is not afraid of sex or the holes in her body.

She is not awed by parents or priests or coaches.

She is not afraid to die.

Say this girl is me.

Carla "Bounce" Reuschel
Dumas, Illinois

Wiggins

Last night we took the Future Pill. It was pink and shaped like a little egg. Bounce put one on my tongue and put one on Orange's tongue and then she put one on hers.

What's it called? Orange asked.
The Future Pill, Bounce said.

On the bottle it said Ergot 7.

Bounce was like, Get ready, chuckleheads. Get ready to absorb some knowledge.

We drank it down with a Strawberry Quik.

To the future, Bounce said.

Me and Orange were like, To the future.

We were behind Orange's house, near the woods.

Nothing happened for a while so I just stared into the trees. They were glowing from the fires. At first I thought there was just one fire, but after a while I think I counted three different fires, then a fourth.

How many men do you think are out there? I asked.

At least a hundred, Orange said.

Twenty at most, Bounce said. Fucking weirdos.

I said, What do you think they're doing?

Orange went, Being warlocks.

Bounce was like, I'll bet all they do is drink hard liquor and fight each other.

I was like, In the winter they're gonna freeze.

Orange said, All the buttsex'll keep em warm.

Bounce went, You would know, Firebox.

It looked like shapes was moving around the glow parts. Maybe there wasn't just men out there? Maybe there were some monsters, too? Like a half-man half-goat or a Bigfoot with a sword, in charge of everything.

After a minute Bounce said, They're trying to stop time.

How? Orange asked.

By living away from things, she answered. No alarm clocks. No cell phones. No responsibilities.

I thought about stopping time.

I imagined this huge grandfather clock on top of a mountain. I walked up to it with a sledgehammer. There was a ladder leaning against it. Just before I started climbing the ladder the clock's face turnt into Denzel Washington and he started laughing at me. His big white movie teeth were blinding.

Then I was suddenly walking into the woods.

It was the fall and my feet were swishing through leaves.

And then I was walking up a tree.

And then it was the winter and snow was freezing my eyelashes.

I walked sideways up the trunk of the tree, my body bitch-slapping science and nature. It was like being in a cartoon without the drawings.

I had gumdrops for eyes and balloon skin.

I walked on top of all the trees, looking down at the fires. The snow was falling right on the flames but it wasn't melting. It turnt the fire white.

Then it turnt it into water.

Then into a woman's hair.

I counted seven hundred and forty-one fires.

And then just like that I was back in the grass with Bounce and Orange. We were lying head-to-head-to-head.

I ain't feeling shit yet, Orange said.
You will, Bounce said, I promise.
He said, You feeling anything, Wiggins?
Not yet, I lied.

I didn't trust Orange no more. There was a coldishness between us. Like when you find a penny in the freezer. I had a thought that I could kill him. I could stab him hard in the heart or cut his throat or drop a machine on his head when he was sleeping.

Then I started dreaming with my eyes open and I saw my soul. It was a crystal egg and it could fly. It hovered over my head. I kept trying to see if it had a face on it but it wouldn't stop moving. Like Denzel Washington. Or like the face of a president or a face that you find on some money or the face of a famous rap star. I tried to catch it but it kept scooting away, just out of reach.

Come here, I said to it. Come here, Soul.

At one point I remember seeing Orange standing naked over a coffee can. He was peeing and picking at his pubes.

My piss is ancient fire! he screamed. My stomach is a volcano and my piss is ancient fire!

His skin looked like it was glowing from the inside. Like he swallowed a star.

And Bounce turning circles with her arms spread wide.

Then all of our clothes were off and then they were back on and then they were off again.

I only touched my Soul once and it burnt my hand.

I woke up squeezing my fingers.

I don't know how I got home.

When I came out to the kitchen Dirty Diana was about to leave for work. Her nurse's uniform was so white. So so so so white. Whiter than Denzel Washington's teeth on that clockface. My head was pounding. Somehow I was wearing Orange's shirt. It said Wrigley Field Sucks! and had the Cardinals' logo on the back.

Dirty Diana said, I'm taking the weekend off.

She'd gotten a haircut. She'd gotten a haircut and she looked like a girl.

I just nodded.

It felt like there was troll hair in my mouth.

She said, Cortina's taking me to Niagara Falls.

I was like, Where's that?

In New York, she said.

I said, New York City?

New York State, she said. It's a voluminous waterfall. It's sposed to be really beautiful.

For how long? I asked.

Just a few days, she answered.

You comin back? I asked.

Of course, she said. I'll be gone a few days tops.

I noticed that her skin looked clearer too.

She'd never used a word like voluminous before and for a second I thought the old Dirty Diana got traded in the way you trade in a car.

She touched my hair and was like, You'll be okay holding down the fort?

I nodded. I wanted her to ask me about my tooth but she still hadn't noticed.

Here, she said, and handed me forty dollars. Don't forget to eat.

I took the money.

She said, If Charlie Chinco comes by tell him the garbage disposal is making weird noises again.

She went over and turnt on the garbage disposal. It made a grinding noise. I looked at the refrigerator.

I could tell that it knew something.

*   *   *

The next day Dirty Diana left with Cortina. He came and picked her up in his purple Hyundai. I had to help her take her suitcase down. Cortina's windshield's got a crack in it.

I imagined them huddling together. The highway wind whistling through the glass.

Dirty Diana smoking weed and Cortina singing Mexican gang-banger songs and maybe getting a handjob.

After I said good-bye I came back to the apartment and took this roll of thick black electricity tape and taped the refrigerator shut. It took a while cause I had to go around the whole thing. I used the entire roll. Being that close to the fridge almost made me puke with afraidness.

Fuck you, I said to the fridge. Fucking weirdo fridge.

Then I went over to the management office to tell Mr. Song about the garbage disposal.

His face looked like it got poured out of a cement mixer.

Bloke again? he cried. I come by tomollow.

As I was leaving he said, Yul muddle owe two mumfs rent.
She'll pay it, I told him.

He was wearing a sweatshirt with a yellow smiley face on it and
cut-off corduroy shorts. His calves are bigger than his thighs and
they're bald and rubberish.

What happened? he asked.
What? I said.

He pointed to my eye. I looked in a mirror on his wall. I had a
black eye and I had no idea how I got it. Dirty Diana hadn't asked
me about that either. She touched my hair but wouldn't go near
my eye. I thought maybe I got the black eye from the Future Pill.

I got in a fight, I told him.
Wif who?
This dirty Mexican gangbanger, I lied.
You ruse bad, no?
I said, I whipped him good and then I busted the windshield on
his cheap-ass Hyundai with a crowbar. His name is Cortina. You
should see *his* face.

Mr. Song laughed.

He said, Yul muddle teach you to fight?
I taught myself, I said.

Well yul daddy? he asked.
I don't know, I said.
He was like, He reave go bye-bye, no?
He was in the war, I said.
Ilaq? he asked.
I think so, I said. Maybe Afghanisland too.
He said, Afghanistan.

He seemed to get a lot of pleasure from correcting me. I never know how to say those fucking countries where the war is.

About my dad Mr. Song went, He die?
No, I said. He just never came back. He was a ranger.

I don't know why I told Mr. Song about my dad being a ranger. I felt stupid. Like my insides were shrinking. Or like I would open my mouth and a ant would crawl out.

He said, Maybe he in Ras Begas winning big jackpot.
I was like, Maybe.

* * *

The next day when Mr. Song came over to fix the garbage disposal he brought boiled pork dumplings. While he worked I sat at the kitchen table and ate them out of a Tupperware thing.

You rike? he asked, poking his head out from under the sink.
They're good, I said.

You eat so fast, he said. Srow down. Enjoy, no?

I nodded and he went back under the sink.

He had this little radio with him. It was set on the floor beside his legs. His calves looked like frozen yellow chicken meat you buy at the grocery store. The kind with cellophane over it. The radio was playing classical music.

I thought about taking the hammer to his knees. It was on the table cause after Dirty Diana left with Cortina I went into her room and made some holes in the wall. Like eight pretty big holes. Then I stuffed her socks and underwears in the holes.

After I finished the last dumpling I took the hammer and went and stood over him. He didn't know I was standing there cause he was busy with his monkey wrench.

He said, You rike this music, no?

I didn't answer and he kept working.

Crassicar music good fol the mind and the spilit, he said.

When he finally saw me standing there with the hammer he looked pretty freaked.

He said something in Chinese and then he just stared at me.

You okay? he asked.

I just nodded.

He said, Why you clying?

I touched my face. It was wet but I don't remember starting to cry.

I said, Here, and gave him the hammer.
I don't need, he said.
Just take it, I said.

He took it and I left.

Well you going? he asked.

I went over to Orange's to check on the Frog. While crossing Piano Road I had to wipe my face like five times.

I fucking hate having to wipe my face like that. I'd rather lose a finger.

Orange

This lady called the house this morning. She said she was from Children's Services.

I was like, What's Children's Services?
She said, An advocacy organization for the protection of children.
We don't need protection, I told her.
She said, Thousands of children are killed and abused every year. Thousands.
I went, Not me.
Then she said, Who's this?
Tim, I said.

I figured I should use my real name with a real person.

She said, Tim Merlo?

Uh-huh, I answered.

She went, Tim, is your dad home? My name is Takada Flowers.

He's sleeping, I said.

My dad was in the living room. He'd fallen dead asleep with a KFC bucket in his lap.

She said, When he wakes up can you ask him to give me a call?

Why? I said. Does something need to be serviced?

Just have him call this number, she answered.

When my dad woke up I told him some lady named Takada Flowers called.

I didn't do nothing, he said.

I was like, I didn't say you did.

He said, People always judging you.

He handed me the empty KFC bucket.

He said, Recycle that, please.

I went, Yeah, right, and put it in the sink.

I think about people recycling stuff and I imagine mountains of rotten diapers. Rotten diapers and Coke bottles with cigarette butts floating in backwash.

Then I went down to the basement and watched the Frog. Sometimes I can't tell if she's sleeping or just breathing and thinking. Her video game was on pause. It was like she was meditating about it or something.

I felt like I might walk over to her and punch her hard in the face. I even felt my hand start to make a fist and the blood rushing down my arm. It would have made me feel strong but I didn't do it. Instead I just watched her.

At one point she turnt to me and said, Can I have a cupcake?

I just stood there and kept staring at her.

The Frog said, I'll let you punish me if you give me a cupcake.
What kind of cupcake? I asked.
Chocolate with blue sparkles, please.
I was like, What about one with nuts?

*   *   *

Later me and Bounce went over to Cedarwood Heights to collect. We knocked on a door that had this big old yellow Cadillac parked in the driveway. This old man answered. He had huge earlobes and he seemed blind or maybe deaf even though he wasn't. He wheezed when he breathed.

You see his car? Bounce whispered as the mummy was letting us in. Vintage Caddy.

He gave us tomato soup and Ritz crackers.

So you're doing God's work, he said.
Bounce said, That's one way to look at it, Mr. Leftwich.

She never forgets a name once she hears it. She says she learnt that from her parents when they're dealing with clients on the phone.

About the soup Mr. Leftwich said, It could use some pepper.

His salt and pepper shakers were two cows with black and brown spots. I could feel what it was like to steal them before I even touched them. I knew how heavy they would be and everything. I wanted those cows.

He gave us warm cans of ginger ale.

Where do you spose this little girl is? he asked, setting the ginger ales down on the table.
I wish we knew, Bounce told him. I really wish we knew.
He said, You wonder how a child like that just up and vanishes.
Bounce said, We live in an ugly world.
They got a task force looking, I said. German shepherds, too.
We all have to do our little part, Bounce said. That's why the donations help so much, Mr. Leftwich. You can be a part of that.
She's allergic to nuts, I added. She'll die if she eats a nut.

We were tag-teaming the shit out of this old fool.

When he went to go get more crackers I took the cows. I know Bounce loved it. I could see it in her sexy eyes.

When the old man came back with the crackers he said, My daughter'll be back soon. You might get a donation from her too.

I started thinking about the Glock and I got a boner. I asked the old man if I could use his bathroom and he pointed down the hall.

After I jerked off I looked in his medicine chest. There was Tylenol for Arthritis and eye drops and hemorrhoids ointment and this stuff called Aricept. I opened the bottle of Aricept. It looked sort of like the Future Pill, so I put the bottle in my pocket with the salt and pepper shaker cows.

When I came back to the kitchen Mr. Leftwich was putting a twenty-dollar bill in the collection can.

Another sucker, I thought.

Bounce thanked him and he shook both our hands. His skin felt like wet Kleenex.

On the way back to the Lexus, Bounce handed me a knife. It was a Spyderco Delica, just like the one she gave Wiggins before summer vacation, but newer.

Do his back tires, she said. Do it.

I knifed the Caddy's back tires and we got in the Lexus.

*   *   *

When we got to my house, she parked and I showed her the pills.

Aricept, she said, holding the bottle.
What are they for? I asked.
Dementia, she said, handing them back. They're for Alzheimer's.

Then she took my hand and put it down her pants.

I love you, I told her.

She said, Just get it over with, Firebox.

And I did and when she came her body shook so hard I thought
she would break the Lexus.

It was so awesome I will never wash my finger again.

When I tried to give her the knife back she told me to keep it.

That one's yours, she said.
I was like, A love knife.
Exactly, she said. Now you and Wiggins both have one.

Bounce

Dinner with Kara and Dapper Dan.

Our dinner table has been dressed in white linens by an Indian woman named Savi. I can't tell if she's our new paid slave or just on for the night. In addition to serving us, Savi has also prepared the meal. She has brown lips and her skin is impossibly soft.

As she sets things down, Kara and Dapper Dan say, Thank you, Savi. Thank you so much. This is wonderful! Thank you!

And Savi replies says, You're welcome, and, It is my pleasure. Her voice is like silk pulled across the backs of your legs. Her eyes are silver almonds.

We eat spicy lamb stew with rice and soft flat garlic bread. There is also chicken madras.

From our Bose Wireless Wave System, authentic classical Indian music drones like a sick animal. There is a flute and a violin riding over the drone. A single drum beats haphazardly. This music could really work on you if you played it loud with the lights off. There is a spell in it. A room that it will lead you to where people go mad and tear each others' arms off.

Kara and Dapper Dan drink imported red wine from Bangalore.

There is not much wine in India, Savi explains. But this is one of the finest selections.

I drink Cherry Coke with Reese's Pieces floating in it.

Savi silently moves between the kitchen and the dining room, bringing in little silver tins, taking things away. She wears a thin peach dress that flows about her arms. She is barefoot and her perfect toes look like they would taste like salty caramel.

We found her online, Dapper Dan whispers to me sneakily.
I say, Is she like moving in?
It's a one-night-only thing, Kara murmurs through her perfectly Revloned lips.

I think she's had injections since the last time I saw her.

Mom, I say, your lips look awesome.

She says, Thanks, Carla! With all the flying, I worry about the haggard factor.

When she smiles, I can see that she's bleached her teeth.

About Savi I say, Where is she from?
We flew her in from Calcutta, Dapper Dan explains. Our Plaxco colleague Vernon Squall used her last month in Boca. He absolutely raved, so we had to get in on the action.
Kara says, It's like having a little bit of the South Asia right in your own home.
Dapper Dan adds, Don't you just love the way she moves?

I think he might be wearing a hint of eyeliner. Every time they come home, something's a little weirder about them. Like they're getting more and more sci-fi.

About the little silver dishes of food Kara says, The spices are supposed to be really good for you. Cumin. The curry.
Dapper Dan offers, Great for digestion, the humors, et cetera.

I haven't seen Kara and Dapper Dan in a few weeks. They just returned from Rome, where they were on a business retreat. To learn how to sell more pills. How to identify sadness from Europe, from across oceans, from outer space. They sent me iPhone pictures of them posing with each other in front of statues, waterfalls, distant Italian hills. I mostly delete them. The ones I keep are for my amusement. I print them out and draw bugs on their faces.

I have dreams in which I remove their insides with large forceps and hang them on a clothesline in front of wild dogs chained to telephone poles.

Dapper Dan says, How's school, Carla?
I say, School's been done for over a month, Dad-o. Don't you remember graduation?
Of course we remember, Kara says. We took all those pictures with the Sony DSLR fourteen-point-two megapixel. You graduated top of your class. You got that creative writing award. For that story you wrote about the alligator.
It was a crocodile, I say. A congregation of crocs.
Of course we remember, Dapper Dan assures me.

Then he says, Are you enjoying your summer?
Yes, I say. Are you enjoying yours?
He says, Your mother and I have been having a wonderful time.
I say, Traveling the globe must be rad.

Dapper Dan catalogs the tour.

He says, Italy, Istanbul, Marrakesh . . .
We even spent a few days in Paris, Kara adds.
I say, But there aren't any sad people in Paris.
And Dapper Dan says, But they love popping pills!
Kara takes a forkful of chicken madras and says, Next week we're going to Tahiti, right, Dan?
Before he can answer, I say, Can I come?
But Kara says, Oh, Carla, it's for business.

And I say, Oh, Mom, I'm just joshing, and I say it just like her because I'm her daughter after all. I sure as shit don't look like it but the fact is I pried myself loose from her perfectly waxed, aerobicizedly tightened, now surgically repaired bod fourteen years ago.

Why Tahiti? I ask.

Plaxco's opening up a division there, Dapper Dan explains. They're flying us out to meet the new hires.

Eating.

Utensils on plates.

The expensive Bangalore wine being sipped.

Dapper Dan says, Carla, honey, can you pass the *badami gosht?*

I say, Dad, you say that with such a charmingly informed accent.

He says, Why, thank you, Carla, that's very sweet. You learn so much traveling. You should hear the things your mother can say in Spanish.

Mi casa es su casa.

That's awesome, Mom.

Dapper Dan: She can say the Lord's prayer too, right, Kara?

Kara says, I sure can. *Padre nuestro* and all that. Then to me she says, Carla, have you been losing weight?

I've actually been gaining, I say. I've put on fifteen to twenty. Mostly on my ass and tits. Wanna see?

Carla!, Dapper Dan protests.

Dad! I protest back.

He says, Since when have you talked like that to us?

Kara says, Oh, she's just teasing, Dan.

I say, I'm totally just teasing, Dan—I mean Dad. By the way, I think I'm gonna change my name.

Dapper Dan says, Oh, yeah?

Yeah, Dad, I say, yeah.

Mom has to spit something in her napkin and set it in her lap.

She says, Change your name to what, honey?

I say, Rebote, and I pronounce it correctly, with a perfect Latina accent.

Dapper Dan says, That sounds Spanish.

I say, It is, Dad. It's totally Spanish.

He says, What does it mean?

It means Bounce, I tell him.

Kara says, You want to change your name to Bounce?

I say, I do, Mom, yes. But in Spanish. Rebote.

But why? she cries. Carla is such a pretty name.

And I say, Because Rebote suits me, don't you think, team?

Then we're all quiet and the music takes over.

I imagine Savi undulating in the kitchen. Dancing to her reflection in our state-of-the-art enormous fucking refrigerator.

Karla: Would you change your last name too? Because we'd hate for you to lose Reuschel.

I say, I would become Rebote Cravenslot.

Cravenslot, Dapper Dan says in a confused manner, hmmm.
I say, It has an infectious musicality, wouldn't you agree?

They don't answer. Instead they simply watch each other. They share unspoken information. The fabrics in their matching Armani suits send conspiratorial information across the table.

With a sweeping change of subject, Kara says, By the way, we received an exciting letter today.
Dapper Dan adds, Very exciting indeed.
Kara says, A letter about you.
Oh, Mom, what is it? I ask.

They place our carefully bought silverware down on our carefully bought plates.

Their movements are synchronized, ceremonious, almost religious.

You've been accepted to Groton! Mom cries through her perfect lips.
And to Canterbury! Dad squeals through his glam-rocker eyes.
And to the Kent School, for that matter! Mom sings from the top of her herb-soothed throat.
Congratulations, Carla!
We're so proud of you!

I smile for their benefit.

Savi enters and clears a silver tin, then replaces it with another containing what appears to be yogurt with raisins in it.

Congratulations, she says in her silky voice, and returns to the kitchen.

Inside me there is a tree falling and it is on fire.

I will climb inside myself and ride this tree to wherever it lands.

The Frog

I woke up with a tail

I growed it in the night like a tooth

brighty got jealous and pulled on it and I felled out of the tree and broke my hand and it felled off and now I only got one hand

the wolves didnt get me cause they was sleeping and the shewolf was busy eating dingdong

she tricked him down with her song and he was weak and stupid

raheem helped me back up into the tree and pulled his hand off and gave it to me for a present he said he would grow a new one cause he ate the right bird egg

but dingdong and shane are dead and the wolves are getting stronger

tomorrow raheem said the snows coming
he knows cause the shewolf tells him secrets that he can feel in his belly

the shewolf makes the snow come with her song
it snows for as long as she sings
it will be freezing and one of us will fall

the one with the orange hair came in and gave me some medicine
they were little orange and blue pills
orange like his hair and blue like his eyes
he put a bunch in his hand and held it out

what are them I asked
wabbit teef he said
widdle baby wabbit teef

Wiggins

At the mall next to the Pinkberry there's a church with a digital Jesus. It's called PlasmaFaith. You can have a digital conversation with Jesus, Allah, Buddha, Jimmy Buffet, or this old bald man called Ben Kingsley. PlasmaFaith's got five private booths and the spiritual magician of your choice comes to visit you on a high-def TV screen.

At Aladdin's Castle I told Bounce I needed money for food. I still had the forty dollars Dirty Diana gave me but I didn't want to spend it, just in case I needed it for a emergency, like if I got bit by a poisonous spider or I had to buy something for the Frog.

Bounce was playing Punch-Out!! She was busting Bald Bull's

ass and all these little nigger gangbangers were watching her techniques. Some Mexicans were watching her too. In between rounds she gave me ten dollars.

That's Alexander Hamilton, she said pointing to the man's face on the money. He was a Founding Father.
What did he find? I asked.
Debt, she said. The national debt. He was a genius.

She asked me where I was going and I told her Sbarro's but I went to go see Digital Jesus instead.

When you walk into PlasmaFaith there's this old lady in a white robe handing out brochures. She don't say nothing to you, she just smiles. The carpet is purple. When I walked in, the woman in the robe was eating chicken McNuggets and playing Space Ninja on her iPhone.

The brochure says Jesus was the Son of God and that he died for our sins and that he could come relieve me of my burdens in digital form. I think burden means body pain, like pain from shitting or maybe pain from blindness, but I figured he would do other stuff too.

What you do is you type in questions on a keyboard and he answers them and gives you blessings. It costs a token a question. Each token costs fifty cents.

All the booths were taken, but after a minute, this woman came out of the middle one. She was holding a bucket of caramel corn and trying to wipe her eyes and eat the caramel corn at the same time.

The booth was small and smelled like those blue triangles they put in the urinals at Tom Toomer.

After I dropped the token in the slot there was all this music and then Digital Jesus appeared out of pure blackness.

Bless you, Digital Jesus said. What is your name?

I typed Wiggins.

Hello, Wiggins, he said.
I typed, Hello, Digital Jesus.

I'm not so good at typing. I don't got no computer at home. Dirty Diana used to have one but she spilled a Red Bull on it. The only one I ever get to use is the one in Language Arts. Sometimes Miss Kimsey lets me stay after class to practice. She has a free period and I have fifteen minutes to get to Science Lab, so she gives me special treatment. She's the youngest teacher at Tom Toomer and I like the way she smells. Like flowers and hot chili peppers.

Digital Jesus said, Wiggins, Would you care for a blessing or would you like to ask me a question?

His voice sounded like it was coming from all around you.

I typed, A blessing please.

Then he said, For whom would you like a blessing?
I typed, For the Frog please. Please Bless the Frog, Digital Jesus.

Digital Jesus looks like this guy in a rock video. From this band called Blueblack Window. Bounce likes them cause she says they're psycho-punk. For someone who died for all the sins of the world Digital Jesus looked pretty fit and well rested.

Then this little piece of paper came out of a slot.

It said, GOD BLESS YOU, THE FROG. MAY GOD BLESS YOU AND KEEP YOU.

Then Digital Jesus said, For an additional token I'd be happy to bestow another blessing. Or perhaps you'd like to pose a question about your personal faith.

I just stared at him.

He said, Are you there, Wiggins?

My mom took me to church once. It was when I was maybe four or five. We went after my dad didn't come back from the war. I remember we had to pray for a long time. I remember all the candles and the statues and how the priest kept wiping his face cause he was sweating so much.

Bless you, Wiggins, Digital Jesus said. Bless you, my son.

Then this music came on. Like violins and pianos and something that sounded like a rocket ship landing on a rainbow. There were doves and butterflies and little naked angels flying. I think I saw that leprechaun from the Lucky Charms commercial, too. That made me feel better for some reason. Then Digital Jesus floated backwards into a pink cloud of bumblebees and got smaller and smaller and disappeared and the screen went black.

And then there was this commercial for Tombstone pizza.

I had eight bucks left so I went to Taco Bell and got a taco supreme and a extra large Mountain Dew.

Lyde was there eating a pretzel. He was standing near the trash. He's so fat he can't fit in the foodcourt chairs.

He said, Wiggins.
I went, Hey, Lyde.
Where's your boy Orange?
I don't know, I said. Prolly at home.

Orange was at French Connection, at the other end of the mall. He was gonna steal this hoody with Shakira's face on it. I think he's trying to make Bounce jealous cause she won't take his nuts.

Lyde said, Tell him to give a brotha a shout.

I nodded.

Then he asked me if I wanted to smoke some weed with him.

He was like, It's the same shit Snoop Dogg smokes. Shit is mad heavenly, yo.

I told him I couldn't and he made a face and kept eating his pretzel. He ate about half of it in one bite.

He went, What the fuck is you kids up to anyway? Copy machine. Digital camera. Computer cables. You startin a business or some shit? Tryin to jumpstart the economy?

No, I said.
He said, Come on, go get blunted with me. There's this little room in the back of Best Buy.

I shook my head and kept eating my taco supreme.

He went, Mysterious little bitch, and headed to Boston Market.

Orange

When we got home, there was a white Chevy Malibu parked behind my dad's car with a bumper sticker that said All God's Children.

Bounce was waiting for me in the Lexus. We were gonna go to the True Value hardware on Hockley Boulevard cause Bounce said she needed to buy a special tool. She dropped me off so I could run in and give my dad the refill of his pain pills I picked up at the Osco on the way home from the mall.

Are you Tim? the woman asked.

I almost ran straight into her. She was standing in front of the door, out of the sun.

She wore a pink T-shirt with a silver lion on it and black jeans. There were big sweat stains under her arms. I think the lion was from one of those Disney movies. She fanned herself with a piece of paper. Her face was wet from the humidification.

She said, Takada Flowers, and she stopped fanning herself and put the piece of paper under her arm and held out her hand and we shook.

She said, The other day I spoke with you on the phone. Do you remember? Takada Flowers from Children's Services?

She was smaller than I thought. Sometimes you can guess how big a person is by their voice. She was whiter looking too. I think she was part Mexican. Her hair was dyed orange, almost the same color as mine.

I turnt and looked at Bounce in the Lexus. I wanted to signal to her in case shit got weird.

Takada Flowers said, Is your father around? I rang the doorbell, but there was no answer.

She was standing in the shade and I was in the hot sun. I had to squint and sweat was stinging my eyes.

She said, He's in there, isn't he?
Maybe, I said.
I can hear the TV.
I said, It's always on. He's prolly sleeping.

Does he sleep a lot? she asked.

As much as anybody else, I said.

What are you holding? she asked.

I said, His pain stuff.

Can I see? she asked.

It's just pills, I said.

The sun was really irritating my eyes. Things got pretty tense for a second and then she asked if she could come in.

I was like, What for?

She said, Just to talk with you a little.

I was like, We're talking right now.

She said, But we're not *really* talking, are we?

I said, What do you wanna talk about?

She started fanning herself with the piece of paper again and went, I understand that your mother has been gone for some time.

I said, Did she die or something?

She said, Not that I know of.

I was like, Cause if she's dead that's cool with me.

Takada Flowers made a face like her heart was breaking into a million little pieces and said, You sure I can't come in for a moment, Tim? It's hot as the blazes out here. I'd love a glass of water.

I said, You're a stranger.

Then she reached into her purse and pulled out a wallet and showed me her ID. It said her name and how she was an official employee of the state of Illinois, in the Division of Children's Services.

I went, You can make stuff like that with a copy machine.

She said, But I didn't.

I was like, You're still a stranger.

She looked at me and smiled. One of her teeth was gold. I thought maybe I could knock it out and give it to Wiggins.

She said, I'd like to help you, Tim.

I was like, I don't need no help.

Then she said, I'm aware of your father's condition. He must be in a lot of pain.

Maybe he is, I said.

Then she made her eyes all serious and squinty.

She said, Well, since you're obviously not going to invite me in can I at least ask you a question?

I was like, I'm sort of in a hurry. What?

She went, Do you feel like you're getting everything you need?

I said, Yeah.

She said, Do you feel you're receiving proper care? Food? Clothing? Responsible parenting?

I was like, I eat.

What about the other stuff? she asked.

I got clothes, I said.

When was the last time those were washed? she said, pointing to my Hoya shorts.

I don't know, I said. I wash 'em.

She said, You like Georgetown?

Maybe, I said.

She was like, You wanna be a Hoya?
Maybe, I said again. They got a good hoops squad.
She said, I've smelled cleaner clothes.

That made me want to do bad shit to her. That's what started the badness in me.

She looked up at one of our windows.

She said, You sure I can't come in for a minute?

Then I opened the door and went inside and closed it on her face. I stayed there on the other side of the door till I could hear her walking away.

My dad was in the living room, asleep with the TV on. He'd been watching the Home Shopping Network. Someone was trying to sell a cat made of perfect crystal. It was called the Crystal Cat and it was sposed to be a great addition to the collection we didn't have.

My dad's head was rolled forward on his chest and he was snoring.

I put his pills on the kitchen table.

I didn't bother checking on the Frog cause that woman had wasted so much of my fucking time and Bounce was prolly already pissed. Besides, I knew Wiggins was planning on coming by to feed her later.

When I got in the Lexus Bounce was like, What did Tyler Perry want?

I said, She said she wanted to help me.

Where was she from? Bounce asked.

Children's Services, I said.

I told her how she wanted to know if I thought I was getting proper care.

Bounce made a fart noise with her mouth.

Proper care, she said. Was she doing stand-up?

*　*　*

On the way to True Value hardware we saw the white Malibu parked in front of the RadioShack on Flint Boulevard.

That's her, I said. That's her car.

Bounce said, Hot bumper sticker. All God's Chirren.

We parked a few cars away and waited for her to come out of the RadioShack and then we followed her.

Proper care, Bounce kept saying under breath. Proper fucking care.

We followed her downtown to the building where she worked.

We followed her to the grocery store and to the post office and to the library.

Then we followed her home.

She lives in a shitty part of town. Much shittier than where me and Wiggins live. It's like gangbangers everywhere. Gangbangers and old homeless crack niggers and wild dogs. I wouldn't get out of the car unless I had to.

Bounce made me write down Takada Flowers' address in this little spiral notebook. She lives at two-fifty-seven Triche Street in this little apartment building with a barbecue grill and a picnic table in front of it. There's a fake stone pitbull chained to the picnic table. Someone spray-painted a Latin Kings symbol on it.

Bounce said, This makes Piano Road look like Santa's Village.

After that we went back to True Value hardware on Flint Boulevard and bought some tools.

Bounce bought a hammer.

I asked her what it was for and she said, Hammering.

She told me to get a tool, too, so I got some pliers.

What's that for? she asked.

Proper care, I said.

Originally the hammer was sposed to be for Sophia George, this little rich anorexia ho from Bounce's Honors English class. She'd just gotten accepted into some special music school in Cleveland and Bounce wanted to break her hands before she left. But that all changed after Takada Flowers came by.

About the hammer Bounce said, I'll warm it up on our new friend.

* * *

That night I went down to the basement and pulled things out of the wall with my new pliers. The Frog watched me with her big buggy eyes.

I was like, What?

But she didn't say nothing.

So I pulled some staples out of a wooden beam.

I perfected my grip and pulled six nails out of the wall behind the washer-dryer unit.

Proper care, I thought. Proper care.

Then I went over to the Frog and made her take more Aricept pills.

Here, take more of these, I said. They'll make you feel less demented.

I gave her some with a cup of milk.

* * *

The next night we waited for Takada Flowers at her house. I was nervous about it but Bounce was like, The cops don't want to bother with Triche Street. They get paid to keep all the thugs from that part of the city out of *my* neighborhood.

It was the hottest night of the summer. During the ride over, the man on the radio said it was a hundred and one degrees and the humidification was fucking madness. It was like five-fifteen. Bounce wouldn't turn the air conditioner on cause she said we needed to think like the heat.

While she was driving, she handed Wiggins a screwdriver.

What's this for? he asked.
Just take it, she said. It's the night of tools. Tools for all the fools.

He took it and put it in his sock. Wiggins wears his socks high and tight like a cheerleader.

Be ready, I said to him.
He went, For what?
To change the world, Bounce said.
I said, Just be ready, chucklehead.

We only had to wait for Takada Flowers for like ten minutes. She parked her Malibu and came out of her car with two big bags of groceries. Her hair looked oranger than the day before. Oranger and more faker.

Bounce told Wiggins to go offer to carry one of her bags for her.
Who is she? Wiggins asked.
Just go be a good boy scout, she ordered him. Go now!

So Wiggins got out of the Lexus and caught up to her right as she was walking past that stone pitbull that was chained to the picnic table and he said something to her and she smiled and gave him one of her bags and he took it and just before they entered her apartment building he looked back at us like, what the fuck?

Now! Bounce said. Let's go!

And then we were out of the Lexus with our tools. I stopped the front door of the apartment building with my foot just before it closed. There was a TV on really loud somewhere. It was a base-ball game. The Cardinals were playing the Phillies and the pitcher had just beaned the other pitcher.

Wiggins and Takada Flowers were on the second floor. I could hear her keys jingling. Me and Bounce took the stairs two at a time, low and wide, creeping like panthers, and just as they was going into her apartment, Bounce hit her in the back of the head with the hammer. Takada Flowers screamed and dropped her groceries and went down to a knee and a gallon of milk fell on the floor and busted open. Then Bounce turnt Takada Flowers' cheap-ass old-school TV on and a Lil Wayne video came on and Bounce turnt the volume up loud and Takada Flowers started pleading with Bounce, face down in the puddle of milk, all desperate and begging for her life, *please please please,* but Bounce hit her again, hard, like three times, one with the claw part of the hammer, and then Takada Flowers went quiet and the blood started mixing with the milk.

Proper care! Bounce screamed. Proper fucking care!

After Bounce took her left shoe, she looked at me. It was a black Nike crosstrainer.

Your turn, she said, panting.

Bounce's eyes was wild. And her face was drenched with sweat. It was beautiful.

There was a painting of Jesus over the TV. It was irritating me so I tried turning it around but there wasn't no nail hole on the painting side so I just let it fall down the wall.

Bounce was breathing hard but it wasn't like she was out of breath, it was like a legend was happening, like she was getting her picture taken after setting a world record.

I took my pliers and reached into Takada Flowers' mouth and started pulling on her gold nigger tooth. That shit was fucking hard to get out cause a tooth is a bone. Just when I started really digging in, Wiggins stabbed me in my leg with his screwdriver. It was my left leg and it was deep like I think I could feel it hit my leg bone and I ain't never felt that kind of pain before. It was like lightning going in me. Like lightning or maybe like a scorpion sting or a shark bite.

Wiggins' face was white and he had puke all down the front of his shirt.

I was gonna give you her tooth! I yelled. I was gonna give you her fucking tooth, chucklehead!

Bounce helped me pull the screwdriver out of my leg. And that's when I got sick too. I think it was cause of the noises it made. Like my leg wasn't part of me no more. It was like it turnt into some chicken. There was all this blood and I could see the muscles and the bone and the gristle in my leg. It was stinging and going numb at the same time and I could smell blood in the milk puddle and the room was starting to spin.

After we got the screwdriver out, I lost my conscienceness.

All I remember is Bounce yelling for Wiggins to go start the Lexus. She was squeezing my hand and yelling as loud as she could but Wiggins was already gone.

Wiggins

I could've used my knife but I know I would've kilt him. Part of me wanted to but the other part knows I'm not no murderist.

I ran all the way back to Orange's place. It was miles. I ran faster than any man and I ran across Farmer's Bridge and I ran past all the crackheads on Sink Boulevard even though they laughed at me and called me honky bitch and I ran through Cedarwood Heights and when I got to Piano Road my lungs were burning and my tongue was going numb and my legs were heavy like I was wearing big dumb cartoon shoes but I ran the whole way.

If I woulda took out my knife I woulda slitted his throat so I used the screwdriver instead.

I know there's a badness in me.

I know that's how I been made and I know it sleeps in the river of my blood like a alligator.

Mr. Merlo was in the bathroom.

Tim, he said. Tim, that you?

I went straight to the basement and woke up the Frog and then I unplugged the PlayStation 3 and packed it in the box it came in and I unlocked her and took her upstairs and we left.

When we were outside she kept covering her eyes, even though it was night, cause the streetlights were bright and the carlights were bright and the muscles in her eyes were in a shock state.

When we crossed Piano Road she kept asking me what was wrong but I told her everything was okay.

Everything's cool, I kept saying.
She said, where we goin, Toofairy?
To my place, I told her. It'll be better there.
I'm sick, she said. I'm sick.

She looked really pale and I could see that she'd puked on her arm. She smelled sour like when milk gets a fungus. I picked her up with my other arm and carried her the rest of the way.

I was so tired I thought I might pass out. It felt like Piano Road was a hundred miles long. Every car that past us was like a monster. I kept looking for the Lexus and I had my knife in my pocket, just in case we had to battle.

Once we got to my building things were a little better, but getting up the stairs with the Frog was the hardest. My legs were cramping like crazy and I thought I was gonna start puking again but I was a man.

When we walked into my apartment Miggy was asleep on the couch.

I took the Frog to my room with the box and I made her sit on my bed and told her to be quiet and she nodded and just as I was about to lie down on the floor, I heard Miggy.

Wiggins, she said in a sleepy voice. That you, Wiggins?

The Frog looked sleepy and sick. Her space alien eyes were still huge, though. She was trying to keep them open but she was losing the battle.

I held my finger to my lips.

Don't make me punish you, I whispered.

The Frog nodded and I shut the door and went out to the living room.

Miggy looked real confused. I could smell weed and Mexican food but I couldn't see the food. She was rubbing her face and trying to sit up.

I went, What are you doin here?
She said, Your moms left me a set of keys. I tolt her I would check on you.
I'm okay, I said.
She was like, Yeah?
Yeah, I said. I'm fine.
Miggy went, You eating good and stuff?
I'm eating, I said.
She said, You ain't having no problems? Nobody been messin wit you or nothing like that?
No, I said.

She finally sat up.

She said, I'm so fucking thirsty. Damn.

So I went to the kitchen and got her a glass of water.

When I handed it to her she said, I spoke to you moms on the phone earlier. She doin real good.
I was like, Cool.
She drank some water and said, I think she and Cortina got married. In some little church near Viagra Falls. With a priest and shit. She sent me a cell phone picture. Wanna see?
When's she coming back? I asked.
She went, She didn't say. Prolly soon, though. Don't you wanna see the picture? She look mad good, yo.

You don't have to watch me, I said. I'm okay.

She smiled and said, You a little man, ain't you?

I said, I'm a man.

A boy-man, she said.

I'm not a boy, I said.

She was like, You messin with girls yet?

I didn't say nothing.

She was like, You prolly are, ain't you. You got them pretty-ass eyes.

I said, It's Niagara Falls. Niagara, not Viagra.

You prolly right, she said.

Then Miggy set the water down on the coffee table and said, I tolt your moms I would take you to the movies. You wanna go see a movie? There's that one with Will Smith where he saves all these blue people. He saves them and they turn him blue too. It's sposed to be mad emotional.

I said, Can we go tomorrow?

She was like, Oh, you got important stuff to do tonight?

I nodded.

Like what? she said. You got a date?

I was like, Maybe.

I can respect that, she said.

Then she drank some more water and said, You need me to stay here tonight?

I shook my head.

And she was like, Cool, cuz I got shit to do. What time tomorrow?
Whenever, I said.
She said, How bout I come by and pick you up at seven. We can go to Olive Garden first. Eat some salads. Get some nutriments in you.
Okay, I said.

Then she put her shoes on and grabbed her purse.

She said, By the way, what's up with your fridge? I went to open it and it's all taped up and shit.
I don't trust it, I said.

She laughed and said, You don't trust it?

I nodded.

She said, You don't trust the fucking fridge?

I nodded again.

She said, You really off, ain't you? I keep telling your moms that you all right but she says you off. I think she right.

I ain't off, I said. I just know shit.

After she left I went to the back and got the Frog and I hooked up the PlayStation 3 to the back of the TV. I pulled the sofa closer so she could have a full visual experience.

When I turnt the game on the Frog held out the bike lock.

I ain't locking you up no more, I said.

She nodded and started playing.

I took the bike lock to the kitchen and dropped it in the trash.

You hungry? I asked.

She shook her head.

I said, You look sick.

She nodded. I felt her forehead. It was warm and clammy.

I went, If you're gonna be sick just let me know. You can puke in the toilet.

She nodded again.

In the game she and three other kids from the trees had surrounded the white shewolf. The Frog's thumbs were moving so fast it was like they had their own brains.

From the kitchen I said, What happens when you get the shewolf?

But she didn't answer cause she was about to win the game.

* * *

When I woke up, the Frog was pushing on my shoulder.

It was morning and the sun was blasting in the window.

Toofairy, she said. Toofairy.
What? I said. What's wrong?
She said, There was a bump in the door.

When I opened the door, the screwdriver that I used to stab Orange's leg was stuck below the peephole. Under it was a piece of the newspaper. Behind the newspaper was a long piece of straight red hair tied around the screwdriver. The hair looked fake, like it was from a clown's wig. At the bottom of the hair was a gold tooth. The hair was knotted around it like bait on a fishing pole. I pulled the screwdriver out and grabbed the piece of newspaper and the piece of hair and the gold tooth and shut and locked the door.

On the piece of newspaper was a story about the woman we jumped. It said her name was Takada Flowers and that she got accosted by unknown assailants. It said that the cops believed it to be a gang initiation crime, most likely Vicelords. It said Takada Flowers was a advocate for the welfare systems of children and that she suffered multiple wounds to the skull and that she was currently in intensified care at Dumas General Hospital.

I turnt the article over and it said YOU MESSED UP, MONKEY!

I think it was wrote in blood cause it was red. I could tell it was Bounce's writing cause she's left-handed and her writing slants like it's falling the wrong way.

I started getting real nervous. My hand was twitching and I couldn't sit still.

I knew Bounce would come for me.

I can outrun most people, but Bounce has this thing where she keeps coming at you. She moves slow but she don't never stop so it's like battling a monster.

The Frog kept playing the video game.

Almost done, she said.

She had all the little kids surrounding the shewolf. They were poking at her with sticks and rocks. The shewolf was making crazy noises, like she was sick and going crazy at the same time. One of the little kids was bent down and he was biting the shewolf in the stomach. Another little kid was reaching into a hole in the shewolf's side and pulling guts out and eating them. What was cool was the kids were turning into wolfs, too, like their ears was getting pointyish and they were starting to grow snouts and fangs. The more the shewolf got feasted, the more the kids looked like wolfs.

I went back into the kitchen and undid all the tape around the fridge and got the milk out. And then I poured some Count Chocula in a bowl and gave it to the Frog for breakfast. She paused the game to eat.

I don't got no vitamins, I told her.
It's okay, she said.

The Frog puked halfway through her bowl of cereal. Most of it went on the floor.

Sorry, she said.

After that I made the Frog save the game at the level she was on, just before she had solved the whole thing, and I undid it from the TV and put it back in the box. Then I made the Frog take a bath. I poured some bleach in the water.

It kills the fungus, I told her.

I helped her with the washcloth and the shampoo cause I wasn't sure if she knew how.

You're gonna be clean from now on, I told her.
She said, But I like being dirty, and put her hand on my head while I washed her.

After I got her dressed in one of my T-shirts and her same pair of pants, we left the apartment. My shirt was way too big but at least it was a shirt.

It took a while to get to Frontage Road. We had to walk past the 7-Eleven and through a dirt field. We walked under the water tower and under this bridge where these three girls were raped by a maniac last Christmas. The maniac's name is Bo Chowder and they say he's still on the loose.

We walked under these power lines that buzz with madness. The power lines are attached to these big-ass metal skeletons and you can see how some little kid got his kite stuck up in one of them.

I was relieved when we finally got to Frontage Road. It was dusty and the sun felt like it was dripping on you. Like it was oil in a pan. The Frog walked most of it. I only had to carry her a few times, but I couldn't go far cause I had the PlayStation 3 box too. I put her down and made her hold onto the waistband of my shorts.

We were lucky that there wasn't hardly no cars.

One slowed down and this lady looked at us with suspiciousness.

Wave, I told the Frog. Wave or I'll punish you.

The Frog waved and the lady waved back.

I like outdoors, the Frog said after the car disappeared down the road. But I like how the outdoors looks on TV too.

There was corn on both sides of us and it seemed like it was growing taller while we were walking. Like it knew stuff about me and the Frog and it had to grow more to understand it.

Don't puke again, I told the Frog.

She nodded and kept holding onto my shorts.

The PlayStation 3 box was getting really heavy and I thought I was gonna faint or maybe go into a coma cause I hadn't had nothing to eat in so long.

I kept telling myself to be a man.

Be a man, Wiggins, I said with my brain voice. Be a fucking man.

After a while you could see the red barn.

I had to go down to a knee. My muscles were so tired and I was starting to feel stupid. I could feel the dirt and the rocks pushing into my weak knee.

The Frog went, Are you okay, Toofairy?

I shook my head.

What's wrong? she asked.
I said, I have a badness.
She was like, Is that like a booboo?
In my brain, I said. A booboo in my brain.

Brains are green, she said. I seen one on TV.

I made myself get up and I made the Frog grab my shorts again and we walked up the long gravel driveway and I knocked on the Poet's door.

When he answered he said, Can I help you?

He was taller than I thought. Taller and older.

His house smelled good. Like food and friendliness.

There were books piled everywhere. They were on the floor and they were on tables and they were stacked high up the walls. In the background was the same classical music Mr. Song listens to.

His big black dog was sniffing at us and kind of whining.

Hey, I said.
Hello, the Poet said.
Can I talk to you? I asked.
Of course, he answered.

I looked hard at the dog's face. I could feel my whole body going yellow like its eyes. I was getting really sleepy.

The Poet said, What's your name?
Wiggins, I said.
He went, Are you okay, Wiggins?

What's your dog's name? I asked.
I call him Doc, the Poet answered.
I was like, Doc.
He said, Doc's a good boy, aren't you, Doc?

This is the Frog, I said.
Hello, he said to her. Hello, Frog.

The Frog was hiding behind my arm.

She's pretty shy, I said. I had to fix her T-shirt cause it was falling
off her shoulder.
Is she your little sister? he asked.

He was smiling now. His teeth were crooked and gray.

She's just a friend, I explained.
Where are you two from? he asked.
Dumas, I told him.
He said, What are you two doing all the way out here?
I said, We were just walking.
Going anywhere particular? he asked.
Not really, I answered.
Just your typical early evening stroll?

I nodded. I was feeling yellower and yellower. I was surprised at
how nice the dog was.

What's in the box? the Poet asked.

I said, This game she plays.
To the Frog he said, You like games?

She nodded all shy and sweet.

There were some seriously nice smells coming from inside his house. My stomach growled.

Your house smells good, I told him.
He went, I'm making chili, would you care for some? Chili and homemade cornbread.

I shook my head.

I really wanted some food but I knew I couldn't eat. It would've made me puke.

I said, Will you take her?

He looked pretty confused when I asked him that.

He was like, *Take* her? Take her where?
Inside, I said. Take her inside.

Then he looked at her and looked at me and got even more confused.

He said, It's Wiggins, right?

I nodded. I couldn't hold the box much longer.

The Poet said, What exactly is going on here, Wiggins?
Please, I said. Just take her. She needs someone. She's sick.

Then the Poet squatted down so he was face-to-face with her. His head was huge next to hers. Then he felt her forehead and looked at his hand.

He said, Would you like to come inside, Froggy?
Just Frog, I said.
Would you like to come inside, Frog?

She looked at me. I nodded at her and then to the Poet she said, Is your dog a woof?
No, he's just a dog, he answered.

Then he offered his hand and she took it.

Here, I said, pushing the box toward him. She's really good at the game. She's about to solve it.

He took the box and then the Frog hugged me but I made her stop.

She's allergic to nuts, I told the Poet. No nuts or she'll die.

Then to the Frog I said, Be good. Don't get punished.

Then I pushed her away from me and told the Poet to get a gun.

Why should I get a gun? he asked.
For protection, I said. For battling.

And then I turnt to walk away.

You sure you're okay? the Poet called to me.

But I kept walking.

His voice had a niceness in it.

His voice had a niceness and I knew he would be good to the Frog.

*　*　*

I walked all the way back to Dumas on Frontage Road. There were some birds flying over me and I kept thinking they might attack but they didn't.

I think birds and refrigerators got something going on. Some sort of wickedness. I don't like birds and I don't like refrigerators. There will always be a battle between me and them. A battle of badnesses.

When I walked back across the dirt field I got on the bus that goes to the hospital. It's called the Big Blue bus and it's big and blue and you get on it at Six Mile Road, near where this hotdog stand got burnt down by some Crips.

All these old people were on the bus. They were holding onto canes and metal walkers and they looked like they were barely breathing. Like they were all traveling to some place to get more air put in their bodies. Most of them were sleepy-eyed niggers but some were Mexicans and there was also a old Pakistanical man who kept making a face like he was meowing.

I tried to give the bus driver my forty dollars but he just looked at me like I was crazy and told me to sit down.

Where you goin? he asked.
To the hospital, I said.
Take a seat, he said. Next time bring change.

Through the bus window Dumas looked dirty and gray and you could smell the nastiness coming in through the window. Mostly garbage smells. But also fish smells and dirty toilet smells and fast food smells and dead people smells.

The fast food smells are the only smells I like. Especially barbecue fast food like Arby's.

When we passed the church where Dirty Diana took me after my dad left I started thinking about this time when I wanted to grow up to be a cowboy. Like four or five years ago. Dirty Diana bought me a big hat and some boots. I used to sleep with them in my bed and I would dream about cows and horses and cactuses.

Once I got asked this question by a guidance counselor at Tom Toomer. His name was Mr. Berg and he hardly opened his mouth when he spoke.

He said, Wiggins, what do want to do with your life?
I said, I used to want to be a cowboy.
He was like, But you don't anymore?
No, I said. Not no more.
Why not? he asked.

The only thing I could think of to say was, Cause they don't got the Internet.

*   *   *

At the hospital I showed the woman at the front desk the newspaper article about Takada Flowers.

She said, Are you one of Ms. Flowers' case children?

I nodded.

Then she called someone on her phone and another nurse came out and got me and took me to her room. The nurse was really tall and smelled like bleach.

Do you have a fungus? I asked her.
I don't think so, she said. Why?
But I didn't answer her.

When we entered Takada Flowers' room there was a old nigger man sitting next to her bed. He was reading the Bible. He looked up at me when I entered.

It was nice and cool in the room. I thought if I got hurt and had to go to the hospital at least there'd be air conditioning.

She's not conscious, the nurse explained.

She said her head wounds were very severe and to not touch her and then she left me there with the old nigger.

Her head was all bandaged and there was a tube in her nose and some plastic bags hanging over her on a metal rack. One had silverish liquid and another had yellowish liquid. I kept staring at them. For some reason I thought maybe you could put a goldfish in each one and this would somehow help battle a fungus. The goldfish would battle it better than bleach would.

The old nigger said, You one of Takada's boys?

His voice was deep and tired.

I nodded.

He said, She's always talkin about her boys. How much she loves you all. White boys, black boys, Mexican boys. Don't matter to her.

I just kept looking at her face. It was really swelled up. The machines next to her were beeping and making little lights.

Take a seat, the old nigger said, and pushed a chair at me.

I sat.

I was like three feet away from him and I could smell him. I could smell how sad he was cause the body makes a smell when it's sad. I know about this cause Dirty Diana has it too. Sometimes you can smell it coming off the couch. I used to think she smelled like a nigger but I think she's just mostly sad.

I said, Is she gonna be okay?
He closed his Bible and went, Don't know. Doctor said she might have some serious damage. What we do know is that she's gonna be blind. We learned that a few hours ago. Might be deaf, too. But there's no way to tell till the swelling goes down.

I thought he was gonna cry but he cleared his throat and swallowed.

Then he went, Don't make any sense if you ask me. The Lord puts a good woman like Takada on the earth — a woman who does nothing but help people — and look what happens to her.

He shook his head a few times.

He said, Old Testament says someone's sposed to pay for some stuff like that. Eye for an eye. Tooth for a tooth. It's right here in the book.

I must have looked stupid cause he was like, You understand what I'm sayin, son?

I nodded.

Then I said, Are you her husband?

I'm her father, he said. No parent should ever see their child suffer like this. Sposed to be the other way around.

The machines beeped a little. Some nurses past by the door. I suddenly felt itchy and even sicker with yellow.

He said, Do you have a daddy?

I nodded.

He said, Then he knows what I'm talking about. I promise you he does.

He was in the war, I told him. He was a ranger in the war.
Where is he now? he asked.
I said, He ain't nowhere.
The old nigger man said, Did he die?
No, I said.
He never came home? he asked.
He came home, I said. But then he left.
He said, How old were you?
I was little.
He said, I'm very sorry to hear that.

He looked real tired like he could fall asleep right there in the chair. I kept thinking he was gonna drop his Bible.

He said, So you live with your mother?

I nodded.

What does she do? he asked.
She's a nurse, I said.
Do she work at this hospital? he asked.
I think so, I said. But she's not here now.
He went, She got the night off?
I said, She's in a waterfall. It's voluminous.

I think that confused him cause he stopped asking questions.

Maybe he could see the yellow creeping in me?

Maybe he could see all the badness?

Then he looked at his daughter for a long time and said, If you don't mind, I'm gonna pray now.

I nodded and then he went to his knees and made a church fist and put his head on it.

I just stood over Takada Flowers. I just stood there standing.

Everything smelled clean and good and without fungus. Like no badness could happen to her. They got so much bleach in the hospital, I thought. They must have like hundreds and thousands of gallons of it.

Then I whispered I was sorry to her.

Sorry, I whispered. Sorry, Takada Flowers.

I whispered it real soft so nobody could hear.

I stood real close to her and watched her dad on the floor, praying into his fist.

I was gonna say goodbye to him but I didn't want to disturb his praying so I opened Takada Flowers' hand and gave her her gold tooth back.

I put it right in her palm and closed her fingers around it.

* * *

When I got home it was almost six o'clock. It was so hot in the apartment I opened the fridge and sat in front of it for a while. My hands were trembling.

There were salad dressings and a red apple and a package of baloney and a box of Velveeta cheese.

The fridge was humming its weirdness but I wasn't scared no more and I even told it so.

I ain't scared of you no more, I said.

You and the birds ain't shit, I told it.

At six fifteen I left a note for Miggy on the kitchen table.

It said:

> Dear Miggy,
>
> I'm not coming home. Have fun at the Will Smith movie.
>
> Sincerity,
> Wiggins

Then I packed my Tom Toomer gym bag.

I packed some toothpaste and some soap and a toothbrush and like five pairs of underwear and some socks and a few T-shirts and some jeans and a hoody.

And then I walked across Piano Road and headed right for the yellow condos.

When I walked past Orange's house I thought Bounce's car might be in the driveway but it wasn't. Only Mr. Merlo's car was there. One of its tires had been slashed and I couldn't decide if Orange or Bounce did it.

I imagined Orange in his dad's wheelchair, his leg bandaged, Mr. Merlo lying on the living room floor. The TV on NASCAR or Dancing with the Stars.

I walked around the house and through the little backyard with the dandelions and the electricity meter.

I didn't bother looking back through the patio doors—I just kept walking right into the woods.

I walked deep into the thickest part.

The trees smelled clean and good and it was cooler there than the rest of the world.

When my legs could go no further I found a good tree and I sat under it. It was good to finally rest.

I forgot about being hungry and I forgot about needing anything.

I forgot about Dirty Diana and Cortina and my dad being nowhere.

And then I took off my watch and buried it in the dirt.

* * *

When the night came I took out my knife and held it close.

I opened it so the blade was flat against me.

There were the sounds of birds crying and the sounds of snakes slithering and the sounds of animals rustling around like children in the trash.

The mosquitoes were buzzing and the spiders were spidering and I could feel all the creatures in the woods creeping closer.

And much later, in the middle of the dark, I could hear the first fires crackling and the voices of men.